AN EMPTY HOUSE

MARGA MINCO

An Empty House

Translated from the Dutch by
Margaret Clegg

U.S. DISTRIBUTOR
DUFOUR EDITIONS
CHESTER SPRINGS,
PA 19425-0449
(215) 458-5005

PETER OWEN · LONDON

PETER OWEN PUBLISHERS
73 Kenway Road London SW5 0RE

First published in Great Britain 1990
© Marga Minco 1966
English translation © Margaret Clegg 1990

This book has been published and translated thanks to the aid of the
European Community.

British Library Cataloguing in Publication Data

Minco, Marga, *1920–*
An empty house.
I. Title
839.3'1364 [F]

ISBN 0–7206–0760–4

Printed in Great Britain by Billings of Worcester

Thursday, 28th June 1945

'I'm going back today,' I said to the woman in the kitchen. She was standing at the draining-board, steam rising from her hands.

'Today?' She turned round. 'Why today? Weren't you supposed to be going tomorrow?'

'I might just as well go today. It's nice weather, it might rain tomorrow.'

'It's not going to rain tomorrow, it'll stay fine, it's going to be very hot, mark my words. Anyway, how are you going to get back?'

I sat down at the kitchen table where my breakfast was waiting for me and began buttering a slice of bread.

'I'm going to hitch.'

'Hitch? With that suitcase?'

'It's not heavy.'

'Why don't you wait till tomorrow? The lorry-driver can take you with him to Amsterdam. You know he's going there tomorrow, that would be a lot easier. Then you won't have to stand for ages waiting for a lift.'

'Motorists have to give hitch-hikers a lift. It was in the paper.'

'There are hardly any cars on the roads. And what difference does it make being a day earlier?' She shook her head.

'None really.'

The woman dried her hands and poured me some coffee.

Of course it made no difference. But I'd suddenly felt I didn't want to wait until the next day. I had woken up very early.

When I got out of bed the sun was shining through the window on to the wall; I always left the curtains open, I couldn't sleep in a pitch-dark room. Light-brown cones and dark-brown cubes with beige diagonal strips on a black background. I'd stared at them every morning for four weeks running, letting the shapes spring up and down and sideways, and then back again until the whole floor began to undulate. I could cover the cube with my foot but not the cone. My toes stuck out over the edge. I walked to the window, removed the cotton blind, raised the sash higher and secured the window with the peg. The morning air streamed in, smelling of wet grass, animals and dung. I heard the man with the rattle. At first it had given me a dreadful fright. It turned out to be the bin-man. You could hear him coming streets away. I got used to it. The other rattle I never got used to.

I lie awake listening for it to start.

'Take no notice of it,' Mark says. 'I can't hear it any more.' But every night it's the same. It's teeming with rats between the demolished houses. Lured by Zuiderkerk, which serves as a mortuary. The guards try to scare them away with rattles. One afternoon I go for a walk along Zandstraat when the church doors are open. Corpses are lying in rows on the granite floor, feet wide apart, lumpy and swollen. Some are in pyjamas, others are covered with rags or newspapers. Two men push a handcart inside, carrying oblong paper sacks with labels on them. 'Another five dead,' an old man next to me says. He has glazed eyes and ears which stick out like small, wrinkled wings. I start hearing the rattle during the day when it's not there.

'We've all counted on this being your last day. I wanted to bake a cake, and tonight Father's bringing back some young chickens. The children have already left. You won't be able to say goodbye to them either.'

I said I was very sorry that I wouldn't be able to say goodbye to the others. But sooner or later I had to go back. She should see it as getting rid of the bother a day earlier. I put a rasher of bacon on a piece of bread, cut it into four and put a piece in my mouth. I chewed slowly.

We decide that later we'll eat bacon for breakfast, every day; nice, fat bacon. I am frying potatoes with onions on the makeshift stove in rancid fat which a friend, Simon, a red-haired boy who was to commit suicide in an attic room on Nassaukade shortly before the Liberation, pinched from the laboratory where he worked. He refused to say what sort of fat it was.

'Have you nothing else for breakfast?' Mark asks. 'It stinks the place out.'

'The potatoes are good and the fat has been refined, Simon says.'

'Give us a fresh bread roll with thick butter and cheese any day.'

Mark pierces a burnt potato with his fork and holds it up.

'What did you used to eat for breakfast?'

'Fried eggs.'

'One egg?'

'Usually two on top of a slice of ham.'

'We never had ham. My mother made me eat porridge. I was a sickly child. I used to hate it. I wouldn't mind some now.'

'Do you know what's really tasty? Porridge with a lump of butter and a lot of sugar – soft brown sugar.'

'I once sat watching a man eating a plate of porridge. It was only then that I thought it looked tasty.'

'Who was he?'

'Someone my father knew. My father had to talk business and I went along. The man was just eating a plate of porridge. His wife said that we had to sit at the table with him. She stood behind his chair waiting until he'd finished. My father lit a cigar and started talking about the strength of the British Army after the retreat at Dunkirk. I looked at the man. He let my father talk on, nodded now and then and said 'Um, um' and went on eating unperturbed. He did it professionally, as if he'd practised a lot. That's how you eat a plate of porridge, I thought, like that man. He had started at the edges and kept spooning it nearer the middle where the porridge, having become thicker, stayed put like a jelly. He carefully divided the last round blob into two before he ate it. Then he held his plate at a slant towards him and went round it again, moving from the edge to the middle. He managed to scrape another spoonful. Then he wiped his mouth with his napkin, stood up and shook my father by the hand.'

'That must have been really tasty porridge.'
'It was ordinary porridge.'

'You look fine at any rate,' the woman said. 'When I think back to how you were when you came a month ago with your narrow white face, there's quite a difference.'

'Yes, I've completely recovered here.'

'You never said a truer word.' I laid my knife on my plate and pushed it away. 'I've already packed my case. I wanted to get off early.'

'It's up to you, Sepha.' She lifted her wrist to brush away a lock on her forehead. Suds fell on her apron. 'Are you homesick?'

'Not really, but I do live in Amsterdam after all.'

She let some cold water run into the bucket and rinsed a towel out. For a brief moment the only noise came from the water. She wrung and twisted the towel. Her hands became redder. 'They won't recognize you any more in Amsterdam.'

I poured myself some more coffee while the woman went on about my thinness and my hollow cheeks and my lack of appetite. The first week I'd scarcely been able to follow her. It had irritated me. It was as if she was deliberately swallowing letters and pronouncing words wrongly. Now her accent sounded familiar, but I only half listened. I could be home this evening, maybe this afternoon, if I was lucky. Suddenly I was in a hurry to get out of the kitchen. I got my case from upstairs and by the time I was downstairs again the woman was making sandwiches for me. She pressed them down firmly and put them in a bag.

I hadn't been standing in front of the house for five minutes when a horse and cart came along. The greengrocer indicated that I could get in. The woman waved me off. At the last minute she'd also given me a bag of apples. I waved exuberantly. I'd promised to write and come back as soon as the trains were running again. I was to let her know when we were going to get married. To Mark, that is. We were just passing. Drinking coffee in the kitchen with the cracked table, drumming on it with one's fingers, flattening cake crumbs, looking for words which one can repeat now and then, looking outside and standing up again, laughing apologetically. We really must be going. Poor Father, missing a farewell again. I used to lie in the grass there and I undressed behind this bush to go swimming if there was nobody around. Yes, naked, I hadn't got a swimming-costume anyway. Let's hire a dinghy. But who says he can sail or swim? Did he take part in any sport?

With practice he becomes very good at sawing wood, faster than the others, he is obsessed by it, stocks up wood for weeks ahead, trunks are piled up, banisters, shelves and floorboards disappear, the house smells like a sawmill. He gets hard skin on his hands. The first time I notice is on my back, hard and coarse. He lets me feel it everywhere and it is a new awakening as if I have another lover who does different things with me, rougher. What will it be like when I get back? What will he have been doing in the meantime? Now that I had been away from him for a month I realized I really knew little about him. I pushed the thought out of my mind while I slowly rode in the back of the cart between the crates of fruit and vegetables. The horse trotted with a regular gait, the wheels rattled, the man on the box was silent. All he had said was that he wasn't going any further than Sneek.

It must have been just after half-past seven; but the sun was already warm. The mist rose over the meadows. The woman was right, it was going to be very hot. The air was full of the scent of water and wayside flowers. Looking ahead of me at the cobbled road I suddenly saw the day lying before me like an unending ribbon full of twists and knots: rides in open vehicles, in rickety cars, with curious or over-friendly drivers, in Jeeps and trucks; having to travel all kinds of roundabout routes, waiting for hours in the heat at the side of the road. But I would come ever closer to home.

Now we were riding past sheds and boat-houses. I saw a couple of sails on the lake in the distance. The greengrocer came to a halt at a crossroads. There was an army truck with a bunch of Canadians clambering aboard. They looked at me as I jumped from the cart. One of them spotted my case and ran over to help me. I asked whether they were going in the direction of Zwolle. He shook his head.

'We're going to Leeuwarden. Why not come along with us?'

He kept his case in one hand and grabbed mine with the other. He was small, not much taller than I was. His khaki shirt was open at the top, his neck was brown. His face, the short nose covered with freckles and round eyes under raised eyebrows, reminded me of a child's drawing. I had to laugh and it gave me a different feeling from the one I had experienced that first day on the Dam. The constriction had gone, as if I had learnt to breathe in a new way.

13

We come out of Damstraat and bump into a crowd of people shouting, moving in the direction of the Palace.

Mark thinks we should stay where we are at the corner of Vijgendam, but I drag him along with me.

'I want a closer look at them.'

'You'll never get through.'

'I've got to see, have a heart.'

'You'll get to see them all right.'

'But now, this minute.'

'Sepha, wait a bit.'

'No.'

He lets me go and I work my way forwards, squeezing between the people, using my elbows and my knees. Mark gets left behind, a bit later I lose him. Somebody slaps me on the back.

'There they are,' cries a boy. He has a white face and hollow eyes. There are red sores on his forehead and his chin. I can smell sweat, the sickly stench of unwashed clothes. I scrape past the faded coats, the saggy jumpers, the threadbare waistcoats. I dive with my head low between two rocking bodies, under arms which will not let go of each other. Sometimes I feel as if I'm being tossed in a blanket. Sometimes it seems as if I'm running without getting anywhere, as if the ground under my feet is slipping away as in my dream. Once I stumble over two legs as thin as sticks in sagging socks. The feet are in some kind of raffia mules. It is a girl about twelve years old. She doesn't notice. At that minute chaos erupts above my head. Everyone starts moving, bodies crane forwards, climb on top of one another, arms are stuck in the air, everything sways and screams. I stand up, I am almost at the front. I see a flat, square vehicle. There are soldiers inside with bronze, green helmets above sweaty faces. One of them is carrying a bunch of flowers. Girls throw their arms around him, kiss him, wave to the crowd. Behind, there are more of these flat, open vehicles and behind them tanks, moving mountains of people, mounted by officers sprouting waist-high from the turret, two small, black discs on either side of their throats, arms stretched sidewards like traffic police. Boys are sitting astride the long guns. Occasionally you can see the face of a soldier through the slits of the armoured cars, black and gleaming as if they have been oiled. The small vehicles and the tanks are completely enclosed by the crowd. I can move neither forwards nor backwards. My hands are clammy. There is a throbbing in the back of my head. I want to join in. I want to shout, to wave, to shake hands. But all I can do is look. And it is as if I see something that is not meant for my eyes. I feel no joy.

The Canadian laughed. He was standing right in front of me. I saw the small blond hairs on his neck, the hollow above his breastbone. I said that I couldn't go with them to Leeuwarden and I was sorry that I had to go in the other direction. He let go of my hand, set my case down and took a couple of bars of chocolate from his breast pocket. 'Take this. My name is Roy.'

I thanked him. He took my hand again.

'What's your name?'

'Sepha.'

'You won't change your mind, Sepha?' He bent forward, his pupils darted to and fro as if they were following something that was circling around me.

'I'm sorry, but I can't. I'm on my way to Amsterdam.'

'Come along with us. We'll take you to Amsterdam tomorrow.' He laid his hand on my shoulder. I felt his fingers moving on my neck.

'I can't. I'm expected home today.'

The others shouted to him to hurry up.

'Well then ... good luck, Sepha, good luck.' He momentarily brought his face closer to mine.

'Good luck, Roy.'

He let go of me. I put the bars of chocolate in my shoulder-bag and picked up my case. I'd seen the cart go off in the direction of the town. The army truck started up behind me. The soldiers were singing. Roy waved and shouted something which I could not hear. The truck disappeared round the bend in clouds of white dust.

The road in front of me was narrow. The trees on either side were set in high grass verges. I put my case down under a tree and sat down next to it. I didn't feel like walking with it, although it was not heavy. I'd never had time to pack. The haste with which I'd had to leave each hiding-place had meant that I'd left something behind each time. Hobson's choice. I realized I was being offered a lift only when a car stopped right in front of me. A man leant out of the window and asked me where I was going.

'To Amsterdam.'

'Put your case in the back.' He had a van which ran on wood gas.

'So', he said, when I sat next to him, 'you're off to Amsterdam. That's quite a way.' He was a small, bald man with a shiny black suit, like the ones I'd seen the farmers in that region wearing on Sundays.

'You're not going that far?'

'I'm going to Heerenveen. You'll be a bit nearer, at any rate.'

'Do you want a piece of chocolate?' I took a bar out of my bag and broke it in two.

'Chocolate!' he cried in a protracted tone. 'Take the paper off.' He clicked his tongue and stuck the half-bar into his mouth in a flash. For a moment he could say nothing, but his tongue and teeth worked fast, he smacked his lips. 'Chocolate, eh? The Canadians, you don't need to tell me, they're real fixers.' He half turned his face towards me. A thin, yellow face with stubble. 'Tastes nice.' He smacked his lips again and began to whistle through greasy lips.

He reminded me a lot of my Uncle Max from Assen, where I'd often spent the summer holidays before the war, who used to let me go with him round the farms in his old Ford. There are bales of material lying in the back. If we are near a farm he stops, puts one of the rolls over his shoulder and walks up to the farm. It's often a long time before he comes back. All that time I stay in the car, waiting. I hear vague noises of buckets being put down, pumps grinding, chickens. My uncle emerges unexpectedly from among the trees, like a dwarf, a hunchback, grimacing and shouting. He throws a few apples in my lap and a handful of nuts. Jerking and jolting down the road, we drive, my uncle laughing his head off at the farmers who have bought the half-bale. 'And what do you think they do with it?' he says. 'They put it away, they put it all away.' Sometimes he whistles, sometimes he says nothing for ages. My hands hurt from cracking nuts. Once he suddenly calls out 'Jews' with a long-drawn-out oo sound. He slaps his thigh with pleasure and repeats it a couple of times. 'We'll be seeing your aunt soon,' he says as we begin to approach Assen. 'Don't forget, we've only visited the farmers.' He gives me another handful of nuts. 'Your aunt,' he says slowly. Then he looks serious. His round, red face hangs above the steering-wheel, his bottom lip sticking out a long way. 'Your aunt.' He shouts passionately, as if he's trying to work himself up. He stops at the first bar we come to. 'Wait a minute,' he says, 'I'll be back in a jiffy.' After the stop he presses the accelerator down harder, his eyes glitter and he cries out again: 'Your aunt.' After about four or five bars he pounds with his fist on the steering-wheel and sings above the din of the engine: 'Don't ever fall in love, for then you're lost, as you'll soon learn to your cost.' When he negotiates a bend I have to cling to my seat. The nutshells roll from my lap.

'Going to visit relations?'
'I'm going home.'
'Oh! You live in Amsterdam?'
'Yes.'
'Terrible goings-on there've been there.'
'Yes.'
'I suppose you saw it all?'
'What?'
'What happened there.'
'Yes.'
'You'd have been better off staying here. It's good out here. We've wanted for nothing.'
'I've noticed.'
'Been on holiday? Makes you feel better, doesn't it?'
I said that I'd been staying with people, holiday was

the last word I would have used. 'You must get away', Mark had said, 'into the country.' And a friend in the Resistance knew people in Friesland who would take me for a couple of weeks. He had to go there anyway, and I could travel with him in the Jeep which he drove around in, even quite soon after the Liberation. I'd been taken from one address to another so often that I went now as a matter of course.

'Have you got relatives in Friesland?'

'Not in Friesland. Look, a Jeep with Americans!' I turned the window down and waved.

'They're British. You can tell by the helmets.' He stuck his arm outside and gave the V for victory sign. A bit later he took a wallet from his inside pocket. 'Open it.' He tossed the wallet into my lap. There was a photograph in it of a group of people. 'That's us. That's my family.'

In the foreground there was a cross-eyed young boy, one knee on the ground. The girls had blonde, fringed hair; the boys, big ears and big hands. The mother, a large woman in a flowered dress, sat in the middle. She looked as if she'd just eaten something sour. The father stood behind her, one hand on a chair, the other held stiffly against his body. There were twelve of them.

'Quite a crowd.'

'And all as fit as a fiddle. None of us are ever ill.'

I nodded and returned the photograph to him.

We're on holiday at the seaside, in the house my parents have been renting for years. The owner is a beach photographer, a large, bony man wearing an open-necked shirt who always has two cameras hanging round his neck. He lives with his wife in a converted hen-hutch at the bottom of the garden during the season and I can hear her doing things in the mornings while she sings in a loud voice '... don't know why there's no summer in the sky, stormy weather. . . .' She doesn't know the rest of the words. She finishes the song, humming, and starts again. My father is clearly taken with her. She wears low-cut dresses, has full breasts and curvaceous hips. He calls her 'a comely woman'.

The photographer takes a group picture of us in the front garden at the end of our last holiday. The four of us are standing in front of the bay window. 'Come on! You must look a bit more cheerful,' he says to me and my sister. That same day, a boy we knew well had drowned. We'd gone for a walk with him along the beach a few evenings previously. The day has been hot and the sea alight, glistening under our feet. There are a lot of us, the boy and I slowly bring up the rear, holding hands. Now and then he stops, puts his arms round me and kisses me on my mouth. Later my sister tells me that he's kissed her too. He was a boy with curly brown hair and protruding teeth. Every time we see the holiday photograph in the album, we're reminded of him.

'It's a nice souvenir.'

'Absolutely,' said the man, 'absolutely.' He put the wallet back in his inside pocket and continued steering with one hand. 'You're lucky we're in Heerenveen so quickly,' he said. 'That thing usually packs up on me.' He pointed with his thumb to the generator. He shook my hand to say goodbye and wished me luck as if he had known me for years. I would forget him as soon as he was round the corner but I would go on seeing the photograph: the bitter mother, the father looking dignified and the ten hearty children fit as a fiddle. A complete family.

The next lift I got was with the driver of a cattle-truck who was going to Steenwijk. He was wearing a blue overall which was spotted with dung and he was reticent almost to the point of being surly. 'Amsterdam? Not exactly a stone's throw away' was the only thing he said. The cab smelt strongly of cows. I could hear them lumbering around behind the partition. I leant back. My head bounced along with every little bump in the road. Now and again I could see bunkers in amongst the trees. Leafy branches were protruding through some of the loopholes, as if a tree had grown inside.

I am not aware that we are going to Amsterdam. It's late and I'm already lying in the box-bed when the farmer's wife comes to call me. 'Sepha, quick, there's somebody here for you. You must get away!' I fling my clothes on, pack my case and throw in the things I have been keeping on the shelf above the bed. The actions are routine. A man is standing at the front door. I have difficulty making out his face in the semi-darkness. All I can see is that he is wearing a hat and that he is fairly tall. He fills almost the entire passageway.

The farmer's wife squeezes my hand as I depart. 'I'll take the case,' says the man when I'm standing outside in the pitch-black farmyard. 'Just give me an arm.' His voice sounds young. The sleeve of his overcoat has a

21

woolly feel. We walk along the road and I feel the wind cutting through my raincoat. I've never been so cold before. The side-road we turn into after a few minutes is even darker on account of the tall trees on both sides. We meet no one. The only sound comes from our footsteps on the stone chippings. I can feel my temples beginning to throb, and my throat and my chest. The man says nothing. We walk along arm in arm in silence, towards something standing on the right-hand side of the road. It's a car. I hear my companion whispering I mustn't be afraid, I'm in good hands. I don't really take it in. Perhaps I'm still in the box-bed and this is the recurring dream in which I'm taken away. I see that it is a German Army car, a DKW, with the rear door open. I'm stiff. Everything about me has gone rigid, my legs and arms are numb, my mouth is so dry that I have difficulty swallowing. I am given a gentle shove inside and my companion comes and sits next to me on the back seat. He says something to me but I can't make it out. I now know that this is how it is done. This is how it happened with the others. I am unexpectedly led away, quite naturally and inevitably. Two men wearing *Wehrmacht* uniforms are sitting in the front. The man sitting beside the driver turns round and asks me how I feel. Would I like a cigarette? The driver says he should keep his eyes on the road ahead and keep quiet. 'You're making her afraid.' They snigger. My companion leans towards me and places his hand on my arm. 'I'll take you to a safe address.'

'Why?'

'It wasn't safe there any more. You're going somewhere else now.'

'Where?'

'There's no need to be afraid. Are you always scared?'
'No.'
'You must trust me.'
'I don't know you.'
'Who knows anybody?'
'And those men there?' I point to the two men in front.
'That's OK. They're great lads.'
We drive along the main road, where it is lighter. The moon appears every now and again, the blue headlights of cars from the opposite direction flash by, pale strips of light from windows not fully blacked out. I can see his face. He has taken off his hat. His hair is combed down flat and is gleaming. His eyebrows are fairly close together. He has a sharp nose, angular cheeks and a wide, dark moustache. A face full of straight lines. When he notices that I am looking at him he takes a firmer hold of my arm, smiles and says that his name is Karel and that is what I ought to call him. And then once again that everything is fine. The wind whistles around the car and tugs at the canvas hood. I can feel it coming in through the door and I'm still cold. The man with the glasses looks round a couple of times at a car travelling behind us and which overtakes us only after four minutes or so. '*Feldgendarmerie*,' he says. Our driver reduces speed. I watch his head, which is now straining forwards more, and the taut line of his neck. The others are sitting in the same way. 'Everything's OK,' says Karel. But by then we are already some miles further on.

We are dropped off in a street in Amsterdam. I recognize the district, it is close to Nieuwmarkt. We walk past the boarded-up windows of the shops in St Antoniesbreestraat. We stop in front of a house in

Kloveniersburgwal. 'Here we are,' he says. I look at a barge berthed in the canal in front of the house. There's a lady's bicycle on deck. We climb up three flights of steep stairs and arrive in a long, sparsely illuminated room, a sort of attic. In the middle is a round table with a few young men sitting at it. I sense that they are taking me in very closely. One of them, a lad in a black sweater, comes across to us. He has the same moustache as Karel though lighter in colour. His face is lean, with wrinkles around his mouth. A lock of his long, straight hair hangs over his forehead.

'I'm Mark. You've landed on your feet coming here. Everybody here is in hiding.'

'Is this all of them?'

'Some of them. There are a few upstairs and the rest are in the house next door.' He picks up my case which Karel had left at the door and brings it more into the room. 'Would you like a drink?'

'I don't know . . .'

'I should if I were you.'

'Yes, give her a drink,' says Karel, 'a double. She still isn't sure whether she's in good hands.'

'I have been sure since I saw you looking at that other car.'

Mark walks across to the table to pour out the drinks. He has a long back which is accentuated by the sweater that covers his hips. His trousers look old and are full of stains. I sit down on the divan up against the wall. It creaks and I can feel the springs sticking through.

'Was it absolutely necessary to come and fetch me in a German car?'

I ask Karel.

'It wasn't necessary. But the lads happened to have a job to do around there. They said: if she's a nice kid, she can come along.' He laughs and raises the glass that Mark has given him. 'Cheers.'

'I think it's quite a risk.'

'After curfew. Don't be daft.'

'Did the swines scare you?'

'Do I look like a member of the SS?'

'Karl the Jew!'

'They'd have you like a shot!'

'Zu Befehl, Herr Sturmbannführer.'

They laugh, and I join in. I don't want to let on that I don't feel very much at ease in their company. So far I've only been with farmers, in remote places, with people of few words. I have to get used to irony, cynical jokes, quick switches in conversation. 'Come and sit here.' They've pulled another chair up to the table for me. The room is lit by cycle-lamps connected to a battery. The geneva, which Mark says they distil themselves, is drunk from beakers and mustard jars. They've given me a proper glass though. Perhaps the only one in the house. There is a mound of dark-brown shag on a newspaper which they roll in turn. The drink tastes like medicine but it is warming. I let them pour me another glass. 'It can make you blind,' the man next to me says. He's older than the others. They call him Eetje. His hair is black and his face tanned. His hands, too, are the same colour as if he'd been living in the tropics a long time. 'And he should know, he's our doctor,' says Karel. 'He gives us prescriptions for the alcohol.'

Around two o'clock everyone goes off. Karel is the only one who goes outside. He's going to bring me a ration card in the morning. A couple of them climb out of the window at the back and go down the fire-escape. The rest disappear to the upper storey. Only

Mark stays. He brings me to a small room with cardboard walls which is partitioned off from the large attic. There's a bed and a chair which has my case on it.

'Do you think you'll manage?' He holds up an oil-lamp.

'Yes.'

'If you need anything else . . .'

'I shan't have any problem sleeping here.' I look at the wide bed and old-fashioned oak bedstead with a quilt. 'Is it your bed?'

'No. It's reserved for our guests. I sleep on the divan in there.'

The lamp swings to and fro and casts long shadows in the little room.

'The one you can feel the springs through?'

'You've already noticed?'

'I sat on it.'

'You get used to it. I don't feel them any more.'

'Did you know I was coming here?'

'We were expecting somebody tonight. We knew that Karel had to fetch someone. But we thought it was a boy, a student.'

'Oh!'

'I don't mind – on the contrary.'

'Fine, then I'll take this room. Is breakfast included?'

'Anything you like.'

'I'll remember that.'

We laugh, he puts the lamp on the floor, briefly raises his hand and leaves me alone. A sackcloth curtain hangs across the opening in the doorway. Giddy and listless I undress. I lie listening until I hear the springs in the divan creak.

'That's Steenwijk over there', the driver said.

It was going better than I'd expected. I'd thought I wouldn't get very far if I kept getting short lifts. Perhaps Mark wasn't even home and I was messing up his plans. I didn't expect you today. He rubs his fingers over his forehead up to his hair, irritably. It's a habit. Sometimes it gives him a red patch. You were going to come tomorrow, weren't you?

My mother has sent me a day earlier to Assen than was agreed. 'They're always at home anyway,' she says. But the shop is shut. I go to the neighbours and they tell me that they've all left in the Ford. It is evening when my aunt comes to fetch me there. 'Your mother just does as she pleases!'

My aunt is a really robust woman. Everything about her is excessive. She has an enormous bush of frizzy hair on her head, large hands and feet and heavy breasts. She sits in the workshop most of the day. If the twins have to be fed she sweeps all the material, thread and pins from the table in one brusque gesture, unbuttons her dress, lays the babies down in front of her and lets them drink simultaneously.

All the while she gives instructions to the girl behind the sewing-machine. She always talks about 'the gown'. 'The seams in Mrs D's gown have to be turned. Are you going to take in Mrs H's gown next?'

Uncle Max seldom appears during the day. Once he pops in shortly after the feeds. I hear him coming in the shop. He stamps on the wooden floor and slams doors. He is always accompanied by noise, as if trying to compensate for the smallness of his stature with the greatest possible show of force. He tosses a roll of material on the table and jerks it loose.

'Here, feel this.'

My aunt stands up and takes the material between finger and thumb. She rubs it and nods. 'That's what I call material.'

My uncle comes and stands next to her. He looks. I feel myself blushing. He is looking intensely at her breasts which are still bulging out of her dress.

'Yes,' my aunt says slowly, 'yes, that's material.'

It was about midday when a car dropped me just past Zwolle. As on the outward journey I was jolted by the rattle of the planks on the Bailey bridge.

I walked some way along the road. It was hot. I was thirsty from the chocolate. I'd already eaten the apples. If I'd had enough money I would have got out at Zwolle to drink something somewhere. Mark had promised to send money. He probably hadn't got any himself. You can expect some in a few days, he wrote in his first letter, he was to get a tidy amount. Next he let me know by postcard that it would be a bit later but that it was coming. It had not come.

I sat by the wayside in the shadow of a few bushes. I could go to one of the farms to get a drink, but they were too far from the road. I might miss a lift. Awhile later I thought I heard something coming. I must have slept. At any rate I lay with my head against the case. I sprang up and scanned the road. There wasn't a car in sight. Next to me in the grass was a girl. She was carrying a rucksack.

'How long have you been sitting here?' she asked.

'Half an hour.'

'Where do you have to get to?' She shifted the leather straps which were cutting into her shoulders. The khaki military shirt she was wearing was two sizes too big.

'Amsterdam.' I sat down again.

'That's where I'm going. I was dropped at the crossroads.' She scraped her feet over the grass like somebody marching on the spot. I could see from her grey, scuffed shoes, boy's shoes, which were also too big for her, that she'd walked quite a way. She must have. There was no crossroads in the vicinity. Her arms and legs were as white as her face. She scanned the road and her eyes, narrow and set close together, blinked constantly.

'It might take some time. Make yourself comfortable.'

'That damned waiting. I could have been there by now.'

She took off her rucksack and came and sat next to me.

'You have to be patient. You'll get there today.'

'Do you hitch a lot?'

'Not if I don't have to. I usually see to it that I can travel with a friend in a Jeep.'

'Oh! I see.' She took off her headscarf. She had thick, black hair. 'This is my first time.'

'How do you mean?'

'Hitching. It's a godsend. I don't care for trains.'

'Why not?'

'I almost fell out of one once. I was about seven, I think. I was going with my father and mother to relatives. It was one of those old wooden carriages, you know, with the leather straps to open the windows and brass everywhere. The door handle suddenly gave, I expect I'd been messing about with it and the door swung open. My father was just able to grab me. You've no idea of the wind that hits you.'

'I can imagine.'

'You'll keep an eye open, eh? My eyes hurt from looking. I'm not used to the sun.' She lay stretched out in the grass with an arm shielding her face. She moved nervously. Her voice was unnaturally high-pitched. I was annoyed that she automatically assumed we would hitch together. She behaved as if we'd arranged to meet there.

'I could have had a lift with some Canadians in a truck this morning.'

'Why didn't you take it?'

'They had to go to Leeuwarden first. They were going to Amsterdam tomorrow. It would have been nice if they'd been going today.'

'Are you so keen on sitting in a truck with Canadians?'

'I got a couple of bars of chocolate from one of the boys. He was called Roy, he seemed very nice. Funny eyes.'

'You don't say.'

'What do you mean?'

'Nothing.' She kicked the grass with one of her feet as if it was in her way. 'You probably think I'm in a hurry? Well then, you're mistaken. I wouldn't have minded staying in Aalten a bit. That's where I've been. Two years. But I had to leave sooner or later.' She talked very quickly, in a sharp, belligerent tone. If we had to wait another half hour, I'd know her full history. I wanted to get on.

'Going back to Amsterdam,' she said. 'I've really not thought about anything else.' She still had her arm shielding her eyes. It was as if she was talking in her sleep. It sounded a bit uncontrolled. 'Mind you, I didn't set one foot outside all that time. It was a very small room with sloping walls. They begin to oppress you. They keep closing in on you. At first I read a lot. Good things and rubbish – everything. But when it started to drag on so long, all I could do was wait. I often lay on my bed all day long. God, it's hot.' She laid her scarf over her face.

'In the last few months I've just walked about normally.' I said it softly, more to myself. She didn't react. I looked at her sharp, aggressive chin, which seemed to acquire a life of its own now that the rest of her face was covered.

'Yes. You won't have had much bother.' She got up slowly and rested on her elbow. Her eyes were almost hostile. 'I couldn't do that. You can see why.'

I opened my case and took out the bag of bread. I gave her a sandwich and took one myself.

'You don't happen to have anything to drink, do you?' I'd seen a bottle sticking out of her rucksack. It was tea, real tea.

'They had everything where I stayed. Off the Americans. Is your family still there?'

'No. I've a friend in Amsterdam. That's where I'm going.'

'I'm going to Palestine. Apparently you can go by freighter via Marseille. Without a permit, of course. But I want to stay a bit in Amsterdam first.'

'Don't build your hopes up too high.' I pushed the bag of bread towards her. She took another sandwich. She chewed, staring far into the distance.

'They said I shouldn't go into Aalten. They were quite tactful really. But they didn't understand. I just want to see where we lived. I want to look at the old neighbourhood.'

'A lot has been destroyed, things pulled down everywhere. You must have heard. We did some of it ourselves. We had to.'

One day in the hunger winter all those in hiding in the house next to us leave to try to cross the big rivers into liberated territory. Mark suggests that we go and have a look, along with the others upstairs. A Dutch Nazi used to live there. He disappears in the course of '44, serves in Overijssel with the army and is shot when he picks up a man from the Resistance. His wife has the contents removed. There is a grand piano and a safe. When the house remains unlived in, it is occupied by the Resistance. Two months before Dolle Dinsdag it is full of people in hiding, most of them students.

I'm last down the fire-escape; I walk across a lit yard and come into the courtyard through a coal-hole. It is a big town house with a curved oak staircase, marble corridors, decorated ceilings and high panelling. Three floors and a house at the back and everything of wood, even the adjoining walls. 'We'll no longer be cold,' cries Mark. The cupboard shelves are the first to go. When the shelves are finished, the doors are taken from their hinges. Next the panelling is prised loose, gilt moulding and all, the skirting-boards, the adjoining walls and the wainscoting in the attic. At night we hoist the wood up. The locals in the neighbourhood, which has already been stripped to the bone, get wind of it by the time we get round to the floor. Men with crowbars and saws seize what we've left behind. They even take the beams away. They demolish the house at the back. From upstairs we can see right through it to the bottom floor.

I told her that it had happened to all the empty houses. I wanted to warn her, to prepare her for what she would see. But she wouldn't listen to me.

'I hope we're there before dark. I can hardly imagine walking there again. Wait, I have two cigarettes.' She'd rolled them herself, fat in the middle and tapering down at the ends. 'Home grown, not bad.'

'What's your name?'

'Yona.' She picked a couple of buttercups and lay down again. She blew the smoke out through her nose, and stroked her face with the flowers. Her eyes were closed as she put her question.

'That friend of yours, do you live together?'

'Yes.'

The small separate room doesn't last long. We tear down the walls and burn the struts and the thick cardboard in the stove. Nobody knows then that there is a colossal store of wood next door. It's not exactly love at first sight. We are in each other's company day and night though. I'm the only one who goes out sometimes. Karel has managed to provide me with a good identity card and I am officially registered. Mark can't go outside, he's wanted. I suggest to him that we both sleep in the bed. I don't just say it because I know that he's thinking about it too. I want to be ahead of him. In the last few years, people have always been ahead of me. Now I want to take the initiative.

The big bedstead becomes a house within the house.

It's the first thing you see if you come inside. It stands at the back opposite the door and near the window with the fire-escape which can never be opened at night because of the rats. If I lie in bed and Mark is still getting undressed I can see them walking to and fro on the sill. Fright stops me from being annoyed at the careful way he hangs up his clothes, creases his old trousers, puts his shoes next to each other. He has a routine. He picks up my brassière or my jumper from the floor. He picks the stubs from the ashtray and puts them in a little box. He goes to the kitchen for a drink of water. And when he's next to me at last, I try not to think of the rat peering inside, its head constantly moving.

'I have a friend, too,' Yona said. 'We went to grammar school together and did our exams at the same time. He often came to our house. I had a room upstairs at the front. I could almost see over the trees by the canal. It was a big room. The whole house was big. When I was little, I used to cycle in the hallway. My parents were out a lot in the evenings. They thought it was all right that we worked in my room. If you call it work. Leo was a randy lad. He went to America about three months before the war.' Once more she stroked her cheeks with the flowers. 'It's taking a long time.' She lifted her head. 'We're not on the wrong road?'

'We're fine,' I said. But I was beginning to wonder as well whether we'd ever get any further. If she'd not been there, I might have started to walk. If need be back to Zwolle. If she'd only stop talking, if she'd only fall asleep. She wants to tell me everything because she knows that in a couple of hours we'll part company anyway. I wish she had another cigarette. I stood up and stretched. My skirt was creased and dirty, my blouse was sticking to my back. I scanned the road for the umpteenth time.

As soon as we were in the centre Yona put on her rucksack and tapped on the window of the cab. We'd been delayed a lot because the lorry which had picked us up at our spot beyond Zwolle had to go to all kinds of small villages and made one detour after another. We sat in the back on crates. Yona had grazed her knee heaving herself up over the tail-gate. I'd not seen it because I'd been making a place for us to sit.

'What have you done?' I asked.

'Damn it,' she cried, 'I'm not as agile as you. I told you. I spent all my time holed up in a kind of loft.' She tied a hanky round her knee. 'One step from the door to the bed. Do you think I did keep-fit exercises or something?'

I thought of the fire-escape which I'd gone up and down practically every day. In the end I could do it one-handed.

'Have you somewhere to go to in Amsterdam?'

I expected her to say it was none of my business, but she seemed not to hear me. The lorry thundered along a road where they'd just cleared away barricades.

'Do you know,' she said, 'at first I didn't know where I was?' Suddenly her voice was much less sharp. 'All I knew was that it was a low house with an attic window above the back door. "You don't live here," said the woman of the house. She always wore a blue striped apron. "But I am here though," I said. "No," she said, "you must remember that you're not here, you're nowhere." She didn't say it unpleasantly, she wished me no harm. But I couldn't get it out of my mind – you're nowhere. It's as if, by degrees, you start believing it yourself, as if you begin to doubt yourself. I sometimes sat staring at my hands for ages. There was no mirror and they'd whitewashed the attic window. It was only by looking at my hand that I recognized myself, proved to myself that I was there.'

'Didn't anybody ever come to see you?'

'Yes. In the beginning. But I didn't feel like talking. They soon got the message. They let me come downstairs in the evenings occasionally, the windows were blacked out and the front and back doors bolted. It didn't impress me as being anything special. Later on, I even began to dislike it. I saw that they were scared stiff when I was sitting in the room. They listened to every noise from outside. I told them that I'd rather stay upstairs, that I didn't want to run any risks. You can even get used to a loft. At least it was mine, my loft.'

While talking, she had turned round; she sat with her back half turned towards me. I had to bend forward to catch her last words. Her scarf had slipped off. Her hair kept brushing my face. Once we were near Amsterdam, she started talking about her father who went with her to the Concertgebouw every week, accompanied her on long walks and ate cakes with her in small tea-rooms. She talked about him as if he were a friend. And again I had to hear details of the house. She walked me through rooms and corridors, showed me the courtyard, the cellar with wine-racks, the attic with the old-fashioned pulley. I knew it as if I had lived there myself. Where would she sleep tonight?

'If you want to, you can come home with me,' I said.

'I shan't have any time. I've so much to do. There's a case of mine somewhere as well. I can't remember what I put in it.'

We drove across Berlage Bridge. It was still light. She'd fallen silent during the last few kilometres and sat with her chin in her hands. 'The south district,' I heard her say. 'Nothing has changed here, of course.'

I wrote my address on a little piece of paper and gave it to her. She put it in the pocket of her khaki shirt without looking at it.

'You must come,' I shouted after her when she had got out at Ceintuurbaan. She walked away without a backward glance, hands on the straps of her rucksack, hunched forward as if there were stones in it. I lost sight of her because I was looking at a tram coming from Ferdinand Bolstraat. The trams were running again. There were tiny flags on the front. Flags were hanging everywhere. And portraits of the Queen. And orange hangings. Everyone seemed to be in the streets. It was the last evening of the Liberation celebrations. The driver dropped me off at Rokin. I'd not far to go. If I walked quickly, I could be there in five minutes. The door was usually open, the lock was broken – less than half a minute for the three flights of stairs. I could leave my case downstairs.

People were walking in rows right across the full width of the street. The majority had orange buttonholes or red, white and blue ribbons. There were a lot of children with paper hats, flags and tooters. Two mouth-organ players and a saxophonist in a traditional *Volendammer* costume drifted with the mass, though far apart. I tried to get through as quickly as possible. I bumped into a child who dropped his flag, which was about to be trodden underfoot. I made room with my case, grabbed the flag from the ground and thrust it into his hand. Jazz music resounded from a bar in Damstraat. The door was open. Men and women were sitting at the bar with their arms around each other. Their bodies shook. All that was left in the baker's window were breadcrumbs. Here it was even busier. Groups of Canadians stood at the corners, besieged by whores, black-market traders and dog-end collectors.

I'd not seen much of the Liberation in the Frisian village. The woman I'd stayed with baked her own bread; she had done so throughout the war and she just went on doing it. When I was alone in the kitchen with her she asked with avid interest about my experiences in the hunger winter. She wanted to know everything about the church with corpses, the men with rattles, the people suffering from beriberi on the steps of the Palace, the emaciated children who went to the soup-kitchen with their pans. I spared her no details. About the recycled fat which gave us diarrhoea, the rotten fen potatoes, the wet, clay-like bread, about the ulcers and legs full of sores. I saw it as a way of giving something back.

At last I was at the bridge. I looked at the house with the large expanses of window and the grimy door. At the house next door, the raised pavement and the neck gable. The windows were bricked up. The debris was piled high behind. All that was left was bare walls. I put down my case to change hands. It was as if, only then, that I felt how hungry I was, how stiff my knees were from sitting for hours on the crate. There was something strange about the houses, as if I'd been away for years. But it could have been that

I'd never stopped on the bridge before, never looked at them from that angle. The barge was still there. An oil-lamp was burning behind the portholes.

Our front door was closed. The lock had been mended in the meantime. I ought to have had a key somewhere. I didn't want to ring. I'd never realized that the staircase was so dark when the front door was shut. Without thinking, I groped for the banister and banged my hand against the rough wall. 'It's nice, soft wood,' Mark had said as he sawed the banister into logs. 'You can cut it nicely into pieces with a sharp knife.' The steps on the upper flight grated as if there were sand on them. I pushed the door open with my case.

There was a black lady's handbag on the bed. A leather bag with a brass clasp. Who had a bag like that? The leather was supple and smooth, except for some creases on the underside. I walked to the table which was full of bottles and glasses. I saw a long dog-end lying in one of the ashtrays. The cigarette must have been carefully put out. Afterwards the burnt tobacco had been nipped off. I found the empty packet on the floor, Sweet Caporal. The divan was strewn with newspapers. Eisenhower standing in a car. Montgomery standing in a car. A new Bailey bridge built in record time.

I had to look among the piled-up crockery in the kitchen for a cup. I rinsed it a long time before I drank from it. I felt the water sink into my stomach; it gurgled as if it was falling into a smooth, cold hollow. The tower clock sounded the half-hour. The house became even quieter. There appeared to be nobody home on the other floors either. Half nine? It got dark quickly now. It was already dark under the few trees left along the canal. I opened one of the windows and leant outside. A man and a woman tottered along the pavement on the other side. They held each other firmly under the arm. They would suddenly lurch forward a few metres, slowly right themselves and start up again. The nine o'clock man always walked there too. I'd not heard him since the Liberation.

'Quiet a minute,' I say to Mark. It is just before nine. I blow out the lamp and raise the black-out blind. 'What are you doing?' he asks. 'Can't you hear anything?' I say. We both listen in front of the open window. A man's voice calls something. It is too dark to see across to the other side, but the noise clearly comes from there and is moving in the direction of Hoogstraat. The man calls out continuously, as loudly as he can, as if he wants to test his lungs to the utmost. Since then he's been coming by every evening at the same time. We can't hear what he calls out. Perhaps he just makes noises. To protest or simply because he's alive. At first Mark listened too. Later he says, 'Oh! That man. Ignore him.' But I wait for him every evening. Once or twice by a full moon I see his spectre. His head is tilted backwards and he cries.

I leant further out of the window. Somebody was coming across the bridge. It could be Mark. He walked like that, with the upper part of his body bent over like somebody walking against the wind.

I see it for the first time the evening before Liberation. Karel comes running up the stairs. 'They're capitulating,' he cries. 'It's finished.' The report has come in at his Resistance army post. 'I'm off again,' he says. 'There might be a fight here. I hope so.' We accompany him into the street.

'I've never walked with you outside.' I put my arm through Mark's arm. Karel has run ahead of us in the direction of the Amstel.

'You look different.'

'In what way?'

'You seem smaller.'

'And you're much paler than I thought.'

'It'll pass.'

'Strange that we haven't come across anyone.'

It's after nine, more than an hour after curfew. It's as if no one knows yet, or as if we're the only ones who dare to venture outside. The wooden soles of my sandals clatter on the asphalt. A window is raised somewhere. We call out that the Germans have capitulated and that peace has come. More windows are opened. A man comes and stands in his doorway hesitatingly.

'Just watch out,' he says.

We cross the bridge at Staalstraat. We meet a group of people in Doelenstraat. A man waving a large bell walks in front. Another has a red, white and blue cockade on his coat. We laugh and shout together. It's deserted at the Munt Tower. As we cross the square, three boys come running out of Kalverstraat. Then we hear shots. The rattle of a machine-gun comes from Vijzelstraat. 'The SS,' somebody screams. 'Scram!' We run into Doelenstraat while the shooting continues.

'Karel was right,' Mark says panting, 'they're not giving up just like that.'

The windows on the canal are closed. The few people who did come outside beat a retreat. We stand in the narrow doorway to the staircase, arms around each other, out of breath.

Somebody else walked across the bridge. Perhaps it was only fifty paces to our door. A man emerged from the hatch on the barge and let the flap fall to with a bang. The woman had had another client. 'An able-bodied whore', according to Mark. Perhaps it was more than fifty paces after all. Perhaps I had to count to a hundred.

Something woke me. I stretched my legs, my back hurt from the planks on the floor on which I'd fallen asleep. The bell chimed. It was too dark to see who it was from upstairs. I went to open the door but the rope didn't work. When the bell chimed again I walked downstairs. There was a policeman on the pavement. He spoke my name.

'Yes, that's me,' I said.

'Here.' The policeman flicked on his torch and illuminated a little piece of paper. 'This is your address, isn't it?'

I looked at the note. It was crumpled and the writing was almost illegible, half erased as if the paper had been wet.

'I wrote it.'

'Do you know who could have had it?'

'Who? Yes. The girl with the rucksack.'

'That's right,' said the policeman, 'she had a rucksack with her.'

'We hitched together. Is there anything wrong with her?'

'She's in the Weesperplein Hospital. She fell into the canal. Fortunately someone was just passing.'

'Do you want me to go with you?'

The policeman nodded. 'All we found was this note

in her pocket. They don't know what she's called or whether to notify her relatives.'

'She's called Yona, that's all I know. Wait a minute, I'll go with you.'

I'd not put any light on upstairs, I couldn't find the oil-lamp. A chair I bumped into fell over with a bang. I ought to leave a note for Mark. Perhaps he'd come home while I was out. But I couldn't keep the policeman waiting too long.

I found my case by feel, took out a jumper and put it on as I went downstairs.

She turned her face away when I came in. There was a plaster above her right eye, her lips were swollen and her hair lay in rats' tails on her pillow. I felt as if my mouth was dehydrated. The corners of my mouth hurt. I thought today will never end.

'How are you?' I asked.

The only thing in the room besides the bed and the bedside table was a chair. An economy lamp was burning.

She moved her head as if she wanted to say something but was holding back. Then I was able to see the bandage on her arm. The sister in the corridor had told me that she'd been injured by an iron object underwater.

'There's so much rubbish in the canals, anything they want to get rid of they just throw in.'

I sat down on the chair next to the bed. I couldn't ask her how she felt yet again.

Suddenly she started to talk, again with her eyes closed.

'I looked through the letter-box', she mumbled the words. 'I used to push open the letter-box and pull on the string if I couldn't get the door open. There was

nothing left. Nothing except a big, cold hole. I
wandered around some other districts first of all. I put
it off as long as possible. I only went there when it
was quite dark. At first I felt all right. From a distance
it looked as if it was still there.' She turned her head
towards me and looked as if she had only just noticed
me. 'What are you doing here? How did you get here?'

'They found the note that I gave you this afternoon.'

'They even look inside your pockets.'

'I'll come back tomorrow.' I wanted to go.

She shook her head. 'Stay a bit. Or would you rather
go home? It's very late already.'

'I've no idea what time it is.'

'How's your friend?'

'Fine.'

'I suppose they asked you if I had any relatives?'

'Yes.'

'What did you say?'

'I said I didn't know.'

'And what else? Did they want to know where I
came from?'

'No.'

'Or how well you knew me?'

'They always ask that.'

'And what did you say?'

'I said, "She's called Yona, that's all I know."'

'That's all?'

'That's all.'

'Just what I thought.' She thumped the blanket with
her good arm.

'What do you expect?'

'Oh . . .'

'You could have come to me. You knew my address.
I wrote it on that piece of paper. I bet you didn't even

look at it. When we arrived here I asked you if you wanted to come with me. And then I called after you.'

She did not reply. She sat up, took a sip of water and ran her tongue over her lips.

I did the same, the corners of my mouth were dry and felt taut when I moved my jaw. I took the glass from her and drank.

She stared at me a long time before she said: 'I had nothing to do. Yes, all right, I could have picked up my case. But it wasn't there, they'd taken it somewhere else. Afraid of Jewish chattels. The house wasn't there either. The door was boarded up. I could feel it. How can a wall stay standing if there's nothing behind it, I thought. It's a sort of deception. As if someone wants to give you the impression there's at least something they've left untouched. Look, there's your house. But one blow from the demolition hammer and it collapses. Then I went to my aunt's house. She lived nearby. There were no windows, no door, the pavement was covered in rubble. I used to visit her a lot. She played the piano. She had small, white hands and she always wore bracelets which jingled when she played.' She paused and tugged at the sheet. 'I wondered where the piano was now. Silly, that that's what you think about at such moments. What's a piano, after all? I still don't know how it happened. I know the neighbourhood. It was very dark, of course. And my eyesight is a lot worse. I never wore my spectacles up in the loft. It wasn't necessary. Perhaps I'd be better off wearing them again. I think I stumbled or slipped.' She shrugged her shoulders and passed her fingers through her hair, pulling at it.

So it was an accident. Earlier on I'd seen her blinking. But she had said she wasn't used to the sun. I didn't know what to believe any longer.

'Doesn't your friend mind you being away so long?'

She had lain down again.

'No.'

'No? What did you say?'

I was silent.

'Were you in bed?'

I looked at the cover moving above her knees. It was a grey blanket, carefully patched in the middle with a lighter-coloured material.

'Didn't you get a chance to talk about it?'

'Now you just listen to me, Yona. I didn't come here . . .'

'I know, I only asked.' She felt the plaster above her eye. 'It stings. I pretended to be asleep for those few hours. I didn't feel like explaining everything. I didn't feel like talking. Now I do to you. Have you seen that little window? You'd think it was a cell.' High in the wall opposite me there was a small window of frosted glass. It was apparently a room which was used only for emergency cases. 'I shan't be able to stick it here for more than a day or two. In fact I'm not badly hurt. My left leg is bandaged, too, but they're only flesh-wounds. I hate small rooms and I always end up in them. Just like in the boat. Before the war I had the chance to go sailing with friends. I slept in the bow or whatever you call it. I had to go in bent double and get undressed on my haunches. If I stuck out my hand or bent my knee I felt the sides just as if I was in a coffin, as if they had buried me underwater.' She pushed the blanket slightly away. She was wearing a hospital night-shirt which made her look more like a patient than did her bandaged arm. Somebody shuffled past in the corridor.

'They could have left me there.'

'It's easy to say that now.'

'I mean it.' Her face bent forward, her eyes suddenly seemed much bigger.

I asked myself what I was doing there, why I stayed listening. Mark would be home. But she held me fast, drew me with her, confronted me with something I had wanted to escape. I sought for words with which to retaliate and I said: 'We survived.'

'So what?'

'That does mean something. It was decreed, if you like.'

'Don't be daft. It was pure coincidence.'

'Fine. Call it coincidence or what you like, but it's a fact. I'm not saying "Let's be happy." I'm not saying "Let's pretend it didn't happen."'

'No, but you got something out of it.'

'What do you know about me?'

'Practically nothing. But enough to feel that it's easier for you.'

'You're making a mistake thinking it's easier for me than it is for you. Why don't you try to see that we're all in the same boat? We're here, there's nothing we can do about it and we have to keep going. . . .' I couldn't. I sounded like some preacher in a pulpit.

'Don't give me that. If I think of my father . . . his whole life spent praying, kneeling to the East. Where did it get him? What was the point?'

'It was his faith.'

'He knows better now. He knows nothing. It comes to the same thing.'

'But it was a comfort to him, he said Kaddish and . . .'

Rubbish, I thought. It was ridiculous.

'Kaddish, or not, it didn't help him. Nor all the others.'

Red spots had appeared on her cheek. Her face was angular with sharp cheek-bones and a sharp chin.

'You,' she said, 'you are afraid.'

'You aren't then, I suppose?'

'Let's stop this,' she said softly. The door behind me opened. 'Go back to your friend. What's he called?'

'Mark.' I stood up, I felt too tired to say anything encouraging to her.

'She has to get some sleep,' said the night nurse. 'You've stayed with her far too long as it is.' She had a brown bottle in her hand.

The noise of my footsteps reverberated in the empty streets. Streamers had blown together in the gutters. I stepped on a paper whistle. From an upper storey came the sound of a child crying. Two Canadians with white helmets and white armbands emerged from a side-street.

'Hello,' they said. They stood waiting on the narrow pavement.

'Hello,' I said and walked quickly past them. I couldn't see whether they were chewing or laughing. Perhaps both. I'd go back to Yona tomorrow. She could come to us if she wanted to. Mark wouldn't mind. She could have the divan. It wasn't for long anyway, she was going to Palestine; or, who knows, perhaps she just said so.

He'd been home. There was a note on the table. I could make things out in the dark better now. I saw the lamp with a box of matches and next to it the letter. 'I see you've come home. I didn't expect you today, I've gone to Karel's, there's a party. Come along if you feel like it.'

I collapsed on to the bed and kicked my sandals off. The bag was no longer there; I could just sleep and forget my empty stomach and everything else. There's nothing to beat good food and drink. That had been early in the morning. Warm bread, fresh butter, pots of preserve in the cellar. Karel would have something to eat and certainly something to drink. He always knew where he could lay his hands on drink. Mark would be there. I sat up. I had to put something else on, spruce myself up. I'd got a tan and I wasn't so thin any more. Mark had never seen me like that. There was still something hanging in the cupboard; the dress which had been made in my aunt's atelier. I'd been allowed to choose the material, take the rolls off the shelf, unwind them and hold the material up in front of me before the mirror. The dress had been everywhere. I'd altered it once in a while. 'You know,' my aunt had said, 'that dress will last you years.'

A faint light came from the windows of Karel's house. The front door was open. On the staircase I heard people bumping about and a lot of people laughing upstairs. A gramophone played 'Nobody's Sweetheart Now'. People were singing to it; it sounded hoarse and worn. Two oil-lamps hung in the room, seeming to float on the thick smoke. Most of the guests sat on the floor, others lay on mattresses, and in the corner people were dancing. I knocked over a glass and broke it. Nobody noticed. I would have to climb over all those legs and look in all those faces to find him.

'Haven't you got anything?' asked a man in uniform. He pushed a full glass into my hand. I emptied it at one swig; it brought tears to my eyes, but I held the glass up and drank again. I spotted Karel in a corner.

I wanted to go across to him, but I couldn't get through. He put his arm round a blonde girl. They kissed. His hand moved over her breasts. Somebody blew smoke into my face.

'Is Mark here?' I asked the man who had filled my glass.

'He was here just a minute ago. I think he's left.'

'Where did he go?'

He'd already turned round. I pulled at his sleeve. He shrugged his shoulders and bent over someone sitting on the floor.

I asked someone else, a man with a sweaty face and watery eyes, one of whose front teeth was missing: 'Do you know where Mark is?'

'I don't know any Mark, love. Come and dance.' He laid a heavy arm on my shoulder.

I extricated myself and walked to the corridor. When I got outside it was beginning to get light. I could hear the birds in the trees. But they weren't trees, they were half-sawn-off trunks with bare boughs. The birds thought they were trees. I didn't feel sleepy any more, or hungry. I could pretend that I was just going home now.

I was standing on the bridge again and I took hold of the damp iron railing. The water flowed along, I could hear it lapping against the canal walls and past the barge. The fronts of the houses were grey. It was dark behind the windows on our storey. I walked to the house next door, climbed the steps and put my hand through the letter-box. 'When I was little, I used to cycle in the hallway.' I felt the chill on my fingers, the chill of a large hole through which the wind blew.

I quickly withdrew my hand.

Tuesday, 25th March 1947

A door banged shut downstairs.

I heard footsteps on the gravel accompanied by the muffled clucking of hens. There was a rattle at the garden gate, immediately followed by a babble of women's vying voices, the singsong southern French easily outmatched by the strident Catalan tones. I carefully lifted a corner of the sheet which hung over the balustrade and peered down below. Madame Ponsailler was standing amidst a circle of her neighbours in front of the fence, with a basket of hens on her arm. From her basket feathers fluttered, clinging to her skirt. She turned and looked in my direction.

'Oui, oui le mari aujourd'hui bien sûr. . . .'

The other woman also looked towards the balcony now. They laughed, pulled at their black shawls, shifted their feet in their black espadrilles, nudged each other with their elbows. A thin woman with her hair in a plait down her back bent forward and whispered something. The heads came closer together, then eased back and a new wave of laughter resounded and a muted choir of 'Le mari . . . le mari . . . le mari. . . .'

The hens in the basket began to cluck. One of the women banged on the basket. Her shawl slipped from her shoulders. She wore a flowered jacket which couldn't be completely buttoned up at the front because of her big breasts. You could see her white underskirt between the buttons.

I let the sheet drop, threw my housecoat over my shoulders and went inside. Little balls of mimosa fell on the floor where I walked. While I had been lying in the sun I had picked a few branches of the mimosa bush which hung over the balcony and had shaken the balls off. They had stuck to my skin because of the heat. I poured water from the jug into the bowl, a white bowl with a brown crack, and sponged myself down. The water splashed all over the linoleum. I put my foot on the mat in front of the wash-stand and pulled it over the wet patch. I dressed slowly. I had plenty of time. If I wanted to I could even go by bus to Port-Vendres and back to see what Gilbert was up to. Are you still here, then? And here am I thinking you wouldn't come again! I can just manage it before I go to the station. He isn't coming until half-past twelve. He may be late. You know the train is sometimes delayed for half an hour or more.

I made some coffee in a pan on the oil stove Madame Ponsailler had put in my room after I had told her that I wouldn't always be eating in the village. It was too expensive. I drank my coffee on the balcony and ate some French bread. The women had disappeared. A gaggle of geese were coming up the path followed by a girl in a wide blue skirt and a blue blouse. She was carrying a basket of oranges. Her shadow, which was short and straight in front of her, occasionally touched the last goose.

This is my first visit to Port-Vendres. The bus has dropped me just where the harbour begins. They are unloading oranges from one of the freighters. The boat is completely devoid of paint and covered in rust. On board, an Algerian is busy with a plank secured to a stick trying to sweep up some fruit which has rolled out of a broken crate. He calls something to the man on the quay. The man is wearing a jumper which is almost the same colour as the oranges. When he sees me coming, he begins to laugh and moves his mouth without saying anything. I walk past him. My back becomes hot. I can feel the warmth from my neck to below my thighs as if I've got nothing on. I go and sit in one of the pavement cafés overlooking the harbour. I can see the stone woman of Maillol with the stone flowers in her hand above the head of the man with the orange jumper: *Le monument aux morts de Port-Vendres*. It stands at the end of the quay. The man walks slowly towards the pavement café with his hands in his pockets. His legs swing as if he is looking for stones to kick. He is taller than most of the men here. His bare feet in his open sandals are brown and sinewed. The feet of a climber. I put his age at about thirty.

He remains standing in front of the pavement café and points to the chair next to me. I nod. The iron table between us wobbles when he puts his arms on it. Flakes of rust stick to his jumper.

'Vous êtes Italienne, je pense?'

He can work through the list, I've heard it before. As soon as I say no they start looking further north.

'Anglaise. . . .' He hesitates.

'Non.'

'Danoise, Belge. . . .' He supports his list with a gesture as if is giving me something. But enough's enough.

'Je suis Hollandaise.'

'Mais bien sûr.' He claps his hands to his forehead, a gesture proclaiming why didn't I think of that before? Though I am dark and the Dutch girls he has met have all been blondes. He beckons to the patron, a grubby man wearing a Basque cap, and tells him to bring a bottle of Banyuls. Banyuls at this time of day, an experience not to be missed apparently. We raise our glasses with the light red wine and drink to Holland. À la bonne heure. For me it is eleven hundred and more kilometres away. The Algerian yells to us from the back of his throat and makes jerking movements with the lower part of his body. Just like a dog. Children with dark-brown legs are standing on the quay eating oranges. The juice dribbles down their chins over their hands. They lick it up greedily. The blue above the white houses on the other side of the water reminds me of something from a long time ago. A summer sky above a tennis-court, or was it a swimming-pool?

He has put his glass down and supports his head in his hands. It is almost offensive the way he looks at me. I feel like asking him whether I am wearing something of his. But how do you make a quip like that in French? He might even misunderstand me completely and we'll end up getting our clothes all mixed up.

I lean backwards, balancing my chair on two legs, my face to the sun, my eyes half shut. I'm glad he doesn't want to know anything apart from my nationality and my name. Whether I am married or whether I've got children, what I do, whether it's cold there, not forgetting what it was like under 'les boches'. He asks only whether I am staying long. He wants to show me the Pyrénées-Orientales, the entire Côte Vermeille, the places where tourists don't go. He appears to have the time. And I'm in luck, it's carnival in Perpignan next week.

In the club-room of the dance-hall near Porte-Notre-Dame Gilbert wraps the red cape he has brought for me round my shoulders. I thought about a lot of things when I left Amsterdam but not about packing a carnival costume in my suitcase. He's wearing a black Spanish hat and a silk shawl round his neck. A thick cloud of smoke hangs in the hall, which is decorated with streamers and lanterns. A red fez, large sombreros, and tall floral hairdos stick out above the dancing crowd. The band is playing a *paso doble*, a dance in which you take long steps forwards and backwards. It's impossible here, the couples are on top of each other and can't manage anything more than a rhythmic jog. At the edge of the dance-floor a man in white tights whirls round on his own, bumping up against chairs and tables. He has a cushion tied in front of his stomach. When he turns round, Gilbert points to his back, which displays a 69 in large black numerals. My cape smells of cheap perfume. The lining is torn on one side; I can put my elbow through it. Somebody pulls me on to the dance-floor, a man with gleaming hair combed back and a black mask. He inclines his head towards me, says something incomprehensible and blows waves of garlic in my face.

I lose Gilbert for some time. Sweaty hands hold me tight, go under my cape, over my bare back and more. Thighs are pressed up against mine. When I see Gilbert by himself at a table behind a bottle of wine I go and sit next to him in relief. He knows a small hotel where we can stay. It's late when we get there, the door is closed, but he rings the bell unperturbed. The landlady, a small, stout woman in a flowery peignoir, greets him amicably. We climb up the stairs. He has just taken my dress off and the woman comes in with a bottle of wine and two glasses. She puts it on the cupboard next to the wide bed. 'Bonne nuit,' she says. There is just one chair for our clothes besides a wash-stand and a bidet.

There was a knock. I had finished my breakfast. I picked up my errand-basket, opened the door and closed it immediately behind me. Madame Ponsailler. Act quickly. Don't stay talking in the corridor. Don't stay talking anywhere today. Mon mari will be very happy. And me too. That had been already decided a few days ago. As well as the fact that Holland wasn't near Paris but much further north. First there was Belgium. Germany was on the other side, on the eastern frontier. Oh, les boches, madame, we know all about them. In Banyuls I had seen the remains of the concrete wall, three metres high, which they had constructed round the bay to prevent an invasion. It's the same everywhere, wherever you go. They've been everywhere.

She put her arm through mine. We walked along the dark corridor down the stairs. I had to watch out that we didn't go arm in arm through the door, through the gate, down the path, straight to the station.

Waiting for the train, which is always late, Mark is lucky, the wind has dropped. The trees are in full bloom. The train comes out of the tunnel. The ticket man slouches to the exit. He raises his hat and rubs his head with a hanky. His brother and his eldest son were shot two months before the Liberation. He himself was in a camp. A family of Resistance workers. They've told me all about it. Doors open, he waves to me.

The house smelt like a hen-coop. We paused by the kitchen door. She pushed me inside.

'Entrez, entrez!' Monsieur Ponsailler sat at the table with a carafe and glasses and a bowl of sugar lumps in front of him. 'A toast to le mari.'

He half stood up, supported himself with a short fat hand on the table and pushed a chair back for me with the other.

I sat down and watched him fill the glasses.

'A half, Monsieur Ponsailler, it's still early.'

I put a sugar lump in my mouth and carefully tasted the home-distilled plum eau-de-vie, a very stiff one, which was practically undrinkable without the sugar. And even so I felt the warmth rise to my face.

'Did you see that we've made the other room ready?'

Madame stood leaning against the tall sideboard. The glasses behind the windows of the cabinet gleamed on either side of her head. She had a pointed skull and her hair was pulled tight over it. It was kept in place with combs at the back. 'Janine helped me. She did so want to do something for the monsieur from Holland.'

'My husband will like it very much, I think.'

In the few letters I get he writes that he is coming as well and that I have to rent an extra room. At first I intend to write back to him to ask why. But I let matters be. I still don't believe I shall see him here. I

59

tell Madame Ponsailler that he is used to having a room of his own.

'Those Dutchmen!' Monsieur slapped his knees and laughed. His round face became red. His shoulders went up and down. He rubbed his Basque hat which he always wore and from which no hair protruded. Perhaps he was bald. 'Those Dutchmen and their rooms.'

A room in a large house. An old house with high plastered ceilings, long corridors, dark staircases and a cellar in which my mother keeps the pickles in brown kilner jars. The cellar smells of pickles. There are damp check cloths over the jars. Every Friday afternoon a cousin visits us with a dish to fetch some gherkins. Sometimes I have to go down with her to the cellar to help. I carefully take a corner of the cloth and pull it back. There is a layer of white on top of the gherkins. You take them out, I say to my cousin. She fishes them out with a sieved spoon. They've gone off, I say, they stink and they're full of mould. My cousin shrugs her shoulders. They'll be washed, she says.

In the attic with the low beams we play in between the chests and old furniture. We climb on to the discarded kitchen table and look out through the skylight over Amsterdam south, the trees, Vondel Park, the towers of the Rijksmuseum. We see our neighbour, a lady who lives alone, come back from her daily walk. Every four or five metres she stands still and looks behind her. She has been doing that since her dog was run over.

'To a safe arrival.' Madame raises her glass. Supporting her right elbow in her left hand, she takes a sip, puts the glass back on the sideboard and goes to look in a pan on the stove.

'I think I'll be going.' My glass was not completely empty but I could already feel the eau-de-vie in my legs.

Monsieur Ponsailler looked at his watch and, with his head to one side, said that I had all the time in the world, that the train wouldn't be coming for a while yet.

'Let her go.'

'I wanted to do some errands.' I pushed the chair under the kitchen table.

'I have to go as well. Can I get you anything?'

'Please.' I said what I wanted and gave her my basket.

Janine ran to meet me in the hall. 'Are you going to fetch votre mari?' At that moment the newspaper landed with a smack behind the open door. The newspaper boy winked at me as he went on his way. He knew too. Everyone knew. And there was Madame Ponsailler's old mother. She came shuffling up the path, bent forward, feeling the way with her stick. Everything about her was black, her clothes, her scarf, her eyes, her leathery face with its moustache and thin hair.

'Le mari,' she uttered. 'Le mari.' Her husband had been dead for years. He had died after a lengthy illness. There were pictures of him all over the house.

I walked past them and laughed, it's going to happen, he's coming. I walked more quickly down the steep path, past the almond trees with their white blossom, the meadow with the goats, the house with acacias in the front garden, which was where the doctor lived. I always walked past a bit gingerly because I owed him three hundred francs. During the first week of my stay he had treated me for tonsillitis. Dabbing with some purple stuff, taking tablets to bring my temperature down. To my amazement, it helped. They'd started asking why my husband didn't come even then. I was married, wasn't I? Was he just going to let me stay there by myself?

'Madame Sepha, une lettre.'

'From my husband.'

'What does he say – is he coming?'

'He intends to.'

'Is he coming soon?'

'I think so.' I said that he was very busy. He worked on a newspaper and couldn't easily be missed. When another letter came, I said that I wouldn't have to wait long. It was a letter from Yona, but they weren't to know. I said it just to stop the talk. I was sorry I'd ever started. I couldn't face the thought of having to think up new excuses after each new letter. And when the telegram came – ARRIVING TUESDAY MARK – I had another problem. I had to extricate myself from the enthusiastic interference of the Ponsailler family.

I turned into a side-road which ran up behind a few low houses. The hills in the distance were a reddish brown interspersed with strips of green. A hundred yards further on, the path petered out. There were no more houses and no more trees, only lumps of grey stone with hard stalks growing round them. After a short climb I reached another path which led to the vineyards. I sat down on the edge of one of the terraces. I was in no hurry. The train wouldn't arrive for a while yet. Monsieur Ponsailler had been right. But if I had hung about in the kitchen I should have been completely drunk by now. I could just see myself staggering around the station. Plumes of smoke spiralled up from the white and pink houses round the bay. The strip of water I could see was blue-green, smooth and empty but for two flat-bottomed fishing-boats. A buzzard hovered above the stony hill, then made a fruitless dive. A few yards above the ground he shot sideways, his claws retracted. A train whistled in the distance. It was going back inland into the tunnel.

The lights go on briefly, a weak yellow glow lights the faces. There is a sour smell of wine and cheese in the compartment. My fellow-passengers pass the time eating and drinking. I've been sitting there the whole night, in a corner fortunately. Sometimes I doze off. I wake with a jolt at every set of points, my head banging against the hard wall. I use my raincoat as a cushion but it keeps slipping down. We are travelling between Montauban and Toulouse.

'There's still snow in the South,' someone says. 'It's the heaviest fall for a hundred years.'

'It was two metres deep in Prades.'

'That was because of the wind. The wind blows the snow into drifts.'

'I've seen photos. Two metres deep.'

'A lot of trees died.'

'Hard luck for the farmers. The farmers always come off worst.'

'We shan't forget the winter of '47 in a hurry,' a woman says. She's pulled a black woollen shawl closely round her and has a basket on her lap and she occasionally opens the lid to take food out.

I've seen enough snow to last a lifetime. The winter is unending. No end to sorting out ration coupons. Standing in queues at the coal merchants. You're too late, there's nothing left. No supplies. Everything is closed. Mark throws the last scuttle of coal into the stove. The three of us sit round it. Karel has brought a bottle of gin with him. As soon as our glasses are empty he fills them up again. I've learnt how to drink in the last few years. Red patches like blisters appear on the white wall of the stove. I feel the heat scorching my face but I don't move back. I say it's just like sitting in the sun, at least if I close my eyes. And then Karel says: 'I know somebody who has just come back from Collioure.'

'Who?'

'A painter, he's been working there awhile.'

'Where is it?'

'In the South, towards the Spanish frontier, past Perpignan.'

'On the Mediterranean.'

'It's a fishing village where a lot of painters go.'

'It would be nice to be there now.'

'It'll be spring there by now.'

'I suppose it is.'

'Something for you two?'

'How do you mean, for us?'

'To go there.'

'What are we supposed to do there?' Mark picked up the poker next to the stove and knocked it against the bottom flap. 'I'm no painter.'

'What does it matter, you can still go south.'

'And the money, how do we get the money?' Mark

looks up in irritation. He has opened the lid of the stove wider and begins picking out the cinders.

'Why don't you hitch? Many people do.'

'You still have to live when you get there.'

'Can't you get an advance from the newspaper for some articles or something?'

'I'm not quite a permanent fixture yet. That's the trouble. They want to see what I'm like first, can't you understand that?'

'I'm very good at hitching, I'm all for it.' I look at my shoes on which ash has fallen as a result of Mark's poking. I want to know more about Collioure, where it is exactly, how you get there. I get the atlas and go over the map of France with my finger. I follow the line from Paris downwards, spilling gin from my full glass, to Châteauroux, Limoges, Brive to Carcassonne, Narbonne and further along the sea. I am almost in Spain and I go back along the gin trail to Paris, making a circle round it with my wet finger.

'I'd really like to. Let's do it.'

'Don't be ridiculous – how can we? Anyway, I've no time. How can I get away?'

'You don't want to get away.'

I understand. He doesn't want to, he wants to stay in Amsterdam. There are important things to do; he has said that often enough already. But he means something different now than in the hunger winter when we only had each other, always sitting together, spending whole days in the big bed, creeping together in the hideaway when there was a razzia, sharing the fear and the relief afterwards and talking, talking about what we'd do after the war, how we'd live, where we'd go.

One day there is a ring at the door. There's an old

man standing at the bottom of the stairs. He puts down a jute bag and hands me a note. He's wearing red knitted mittens and a black cap. The bag contains potatoes, an envelope with ration cards and a hundred-guilder note. I discover this only after the man has left. I run after him, catch up with him on the bridge and ask him where it comes from. He stops briefly and points upwards with his knitted thumb. 'From the dear Lord,' he says and continues walking. As I thank the dear Lord on my way upstairs I realize that it is the first time in my life I have done so and I go in waving the hundred-guilder note.

'Now we can do what we like,' I say. 'We can go and eat out tonight ... I've got ration cards as well. Where shall we go?'

'To Freek's in Spuistraat. Apparently you can still get steak there for forty guilders or so.'

'Or Chinese.'

'Yes, a nice piece of chicken. It's cat or dog, of course, but you don't taste it if they don't tell you.'

'You have to go to Kempinski's for game.'

'The famous jugged hare.'

'Fried sole at Rienstra – what about that?'

'Lobster.'

We eat at home as usual, by the light of wicks floating in rape-seed oil. The battery is empty.

'Things are looking up,' I say as we sit on the mattress after having eaten, our legs under a blanket. 'Potatoes, ration cards and money from our dear Lord and the Russians past Danzig.'

Mark strokes my back. 'A little more patience and then you'll really see something.'

At first he wants to know why I don't join in, why I don't tag along, going from one party to another with loads of drink and English cigarettes, waking up in strange beds next to people you don't know. 'This is what we've been waiting for, isn't it?' Later he takes it for granted that I stay at home.

I stuff the Red Cross announcements bringing news of the death of my parents and my sister and the name of the camp and the date in a drawer. I cover the letters with other papers like somebody throwing a spadeful of sand into a hole. Sometimes I stand in front of the drawer without opening it. What is it I want? Now I know for certain. I can't deceive myself any more. It seems to fit into my scheme of things that Mark stays away more and more often. I do nothing about it.

'Still, you ought to give it a try,' Karel says. He tops up the glasses and puts the bottle behind his chair away from the heat of the stove. 'Think about it.'

'How did you get hold of the gin?'

'From a dealer I know well.'

'You seem to know everybody.'

'I don't need a holiday. I've been doing nothing for long enough.'

'You needn't do nothing there.'

'It's different for painters. They need a change of atmosphere.'

'Me too.' Again I spill the gin and again my finger traces a path over the atlas.

'This is the best time to go.'

'It's easy for you to talk.'

'I'll go alone.' I look at the damp lines on the map of France and empty my glass. I can go alone; I can pack my case and say: ' 'Bye for now, I'll be seeing you.' Nobody can stop me. I'm already standing on the road to The Hague, where I get a lift to the frontier.

I'll be in Paris by evening, no problem. I can't keep still. I walk from one end of the room to the other, shouting a few times that I'm off, kick the back end of the bed, bang into the table and push down the round top which is not securely fixed. My scalp is getting hot. It tingles under my hair. I go and sit by the window, look out at the frozen canal and say I've had enough of this cold town with the piles of snow lying in hard ridges along the pavement; enough of the lifeless trees, the decrepit houses with boarded-up windows. I should never have come back to Amsterdam, and because they say nothing and don't look at me I shout that I'm going to lie on a warm beach on the Côte Vermeille or whatever it's called. I keep on shouting and at the same time notice that, if you shout hard enough, people listen and nobody contradicts you. I jump up and I ask why people act as if nothing has happened, why they object to the fact that you're still there. I want to go on but Mark says: 'You're drunk.' He says it calmly, simply observing a fact. He hasn't turned round, although at that moment I'm standing behind him. His hair hangs down his neck. There's a crease across the back of his jacket, which is too big for him.

Karel pulls at my arm. 'Just calm down.'

'Calm down?' I can sense that my face is red, my skin is tingling.

'I don't know why you get in such a state,' Mark says. He rubs his fingers over his forehead.

'What do you know, then?'

'What do you want? To be pitied, nursed?'

I am still standing behind him. He sits bent forward with his arms on his knees. I want to say yes, and at the same time no. But I can't get a word out. Maybe he's right. I don't make it easy for him. Something explodes in the stove, as if a piece of wood has been thrown in. It's full of cigarette-ends and coke under the lid. Brown patches have been scorched in the floor around it.

Mark looks at his watch and stands up. 'I see it's still early. I'm going out for a bit.' He says it without looking at me.

I don't reply.

When he has left the room I go and lie on the mattress and ask for another glass. Karel shakes his head. 'You've had enough.'

'I'm not drunk.' I hear the front door close.

'I thought it was a good idea of mine for you . . .'

'We should never have married.'

'It'll work out. He's a bit adrift, but who isn't?'

'One has come adrift and the other has run aground. It's a nice arrangement. Do you think I'm sentimental?'

'Sometimes.'

'We're like that.'

'Who's we?'

'We Jews. We have a number of features in common.'

'Do you think so?'

'I don't. But that's what people think. Do you?'

'I don't see any difference.'

'They think we are sentimental, sensual, melancholic, brooding, clever, strange.'

'Stop it, please.'

'Give me something to drink.'

'I have a weak spot for Mark.'

'And for me?'

Karel fills the glasses. I reach out my hand.

'Can you drink lying down?'

'Yes. Look. I press my chin on to my chest. Nothing

else moves.' I carefully take a sip. You see. Did my body move?'

'No.'

'What do you think of it?'

'Nice.'

'The trick, or ...'

'Both.'

'He'll probably be away for quite a while again, don't you think?'

Karel comes and sits on the mattress. I put my hand on his shoulder. When he bends over to take a sip, his face comes near to mine. He stays as he is, puts our glasses on the floor, kisses me. We embrace. His hands touch my breasts.

'Wait.' I take my jumper off and in the few seconds that my head is covered I feel his mouth on my body. His lips skim over my skin.

A week later I show Mark my ticket. He looks surprised. He's forgotten my outburst and he's not used to my being persistent, to my doing something besides hanging around, looking at the ruined house next door, at the barge in front of the house where the woman receives her clients, and waiting for him till he comes home, till I see him coming across the bridge late in the evening, like the spectre of the nine o'clock man or early in the morning when the mist hangs over the water.

'Where did you get the money from?'

'Borrowed it.'

'Who from?'

'From Karel.'

'What would we do without Karel?'

'He's somebody you can count on.'

'How will you pay it back?'

'From the compensation I've been promised.'

'But we'll need that money here for clothes and furniture and . . .'

'That can wait.'

'Well, all right. Go, then. I'll manage.'

'I don't doubt that for a minute.'

'Sepha, you mustn't think I'm glad that you're going away.'

'It'll be a lot simpler for you.'

'For you too, I hope. Perhaps you'll realize there what you're doing.'

'What I'm doing?'

'You're trying to make somebody feel guilty for what has happened.'

'Do you mean you? Is that what you think?'

'I know you don't do it deliberately.'

I want to explain why I'm going. I want to tell him that what he thinks isn't completely wrong, but it's as if we're never allowed to talk about these things, there's always an interruption.

At that moment Tinka comes in.

'The door was open.'

'Yes, the catch is broken again.'

'Aren't you ready yet?'

'Almost.' He's tying his tie. 'I'll be with you in a minute.'

As Tinka walks to the window I sit on one knee in front of the stove. Her shoes are immaculately clean as if she hasn't set foot out of doors. The seams of her nylons are straight as a die. I break up the chunks of coke with the poker until I can see a glow again. I hear Mark mumble something about a handkerchief he can't find. Tinka leans on the window-sill.

'Nice view from here.'

'Haven't you seen it before?' I stand up.

'Not with snow.'

'I often look out at it.'

'I can believe that.'

'I never get tired of it.'

'Does somebody live on that barge? Smoke is coming out of the chimney.'

'A woman lives there who goes to bed with everybody. For money. She's just a whore.'

'Who?' Mark buttons his coat up.

'Our neighbour across the way.'

'Oh, that slut.' He walks to the door. 'Well, we'll be off if you don't mind.'

'It's a pity you can't come too.' Tinka turns towards me. A round, rather shiny face with blonde hair hanging thickly around it. Light-grey eyes.

'Have a nice time.' As they go downstairs I notice that I've been leaning on the window-sill with the hot poker. It has left a brown mark.

Smoke was rising from the land adjoining one of the houses below me. A man and a small boy were busy burning rubbish. The man poked the smouldering heap with a stick. When the flames flared up, the small boy threw branches and cardboard boxes on to the fire. The blue smoke drifted slowly in the direction of the village, to the line of cypresses enclosing the cemetery. I sat up. I could see a small procession through the trees. Four altar-boys and a priest in black vestments and white surplices. One of the boys was carrying a brass cross on a black pole; the boy next to him, a font of holy water. They walked almost at a canter with flapping skirts and shoulders moving angularly as if monsieur le curé was continually chivvying them along. He was the last to disappear around the bend in the road. They would soon be going through the gate with the silver scrolls, the entrance to the cemetery. I'd been there a few times. I'd walked over the shell path past the sepulchres; famille Soubira, famille Gastaud, famille Camou, famille Rouanet, dead families all together under one roof, behind green-painted iron doors, front gardens full of flowers, cast-iron gates. Death acquired a somewhat agreeable air.

Again I heard a train whistle in the distance. Why was Mark coming?

'Apparently he's living with T,' Yona wrote. 'But I don't know for certain. I've not been to see him since you left. Perhaps you shouldn't have left; perhaps you should have kept things open. But what would be the point? Does he understand you? You're fine where you are. I think you should always give in to something you feel at a certain moment. They don't make any allowances for you, either.

'I've given up my job with the Foundation. That won't surprise you. I couldn't do it any longer. It upset me. Now I'm painting. There's also a commission to illustrate a book in the pipeline. For once, I've got contacts. And I've got a bit of money. It almost seems as if life is becoming normal again, at least if you don't read the newspapers. The Nazis are becoming active in Germany again, swastikas on walls, desecration of Jewish cemeteries. You're all right where you are (I've written that already). You probably won't see any newspapers, and anyway in a foreign language perhaps it doesn't hit you as hard. Yesterday something happened to me which made me think it's not as

normal as I try to make out. I was walking in Plantage.
Across from Artis Zoo. A boy with a basket on his
bicycle, a butcher's boy I suppose, came up behind
me. He cycled slowly past me, looked at me as if he
recognized me and cried: "Hey, Sara, are you still
here?" Of course you shouldn't dwell on something
like that. It's best to regard it as a kind of greeting.
That's what they're like in Amsterdam, but you know
what I'm like. . . .'

Although it's almost a year since I saw her last – that
evening in the Weesperplein Hospital – I immediately
recognize her voice. I call for her to come upstairs
when I hear her on the stairs. I quickly go inside, look
around, move a chair, pick up a newspaper and shove
a pair of slippers under the mattress. She's in the
doorway before I'm back in the corridor. She's wearing
an old raincoat which is too long for her. Her face is
thinner, her nose strikingly sharp below the glasses in
the steel frames.
      'You're a long way up.'
      'Did you manage to find it easily?'
      'Why not? I know the neighbourhood well.'
      'I suppose you used to live around here somewhere?'
      'No, we didn't. My aunt did. She lived on Groenburg-
wal.'
      'Is your house still there?'
      'No. I told you all about that.' She says it as if she
had told me a few minutes ago. She makes an impatient
gesture with her arm, takes her coat off and throws it
over a chair. 'What a dilapidated mess. You know it
used to be a sweatshop here?'
      'I know. You can still see from the marks on the

floor – that's where the machines were.'

She walks across to one of the windows. 'East India House, would you believe it! Still with a man with paperwork behind every window. I often did errands for my aunt here. Fetched cheese from Wegeman, across the road. His wife had a wig.'

'She still has.'

'Fish from the stalls on Nieuwmarkt. And herbs from Jacob Hooy. In one of those white pointed bags on which men in yellow cloth jackets wrote the names. It smelt nice. I was always glad if I had to wait a while for my turn.'

'Why don't you sit down? Mark'll be home in a minute. I wanted to let you know when we got married but I didn't know where you were.'

'You got married?' She takes the chair next to the stove.

'In August. Shortly after we'd been hitch-hiking.'

'Oh, as long ago as that.'

The town hall is only a few streets away; over the bridge down Rusland, around the corner on Oude Zijds Voorburgwal. Karel and a few friends who lived in the upper storey in the house next door go with us. They have different names now. Some of them have shaved off their moustaches and are scarcely recognizable in their neat suits. I feel uncomfortable in my borrowed dress which is too tight. I stare at the copper ring on my finger. It leaves a black mark because my hands are so clammy. Over my head I can hear the voice of the registrar saying a word in memory of absent members of the family: 'But after these dark times which are now past, happiness awaits you both.'

I make two cups of filter coffee in the kitchen. I've been convinced for some time that Yona lived in the house next door to us. But I wonder now why I was so certain. So many houses on the canals were left behind empty and pulled down. When I come in with the coffee she's fiddling with a button hanging loose from her jacket. She winds the thread at the back round it. She has long, bony fingers.

'Where are you living now?'

'I found an attic in Leidsegracht.'

'Is it nice?'

'Yes. Good light. I paint now and then, if I've time.'

'I didn't know you did that.'

'I haven't got much talent. I wanted to do music. When I left grammar school I wanted to go to music school. Nothing came of it.'

'Was the suitcase still there, the one you were to pick up?'

'No, it had gone. Taken somewhere else and disappeared. Have you had any things returned?'

'The odd thing.'

'You mustn't ask too much of people. Have you anything to smoke? I left my cigarettes at the office.'

'Do you work?' I give her the box of tobacco.

'Yes, half-days with the War Victims Foundation.'

'Why there, in God's name?'

'I have to do something.'

'But why there, of all places? There are enough jobs.'

'I thought it was just up my street.' The button is secured again. She stretches her legs, plants her feet on the floor with her toes upwards so that I'm looking at them. They are wide apart like the feet in the Zuiderkerk. 'I've always wanted to know exactly how it happened. I listen to the stories that people come and tell. I put myself in their place. Try to imagine how they felt. It's a cheap way of showing solidarity, of course. One of our regular clients is a girl who was in a whole series of camps. She was picked up when she was seventeen. In one of the camps she was in the experiments barracks. They've messed about with her rather. Her arms and her neck are full of scars. Sometimes I'm a bit afraid of her. She has a hard, shrill voice which cuts through the whole office. She swears at everything and everybody. Once she said to me: "You were all right, weren't you, in your little cubby-hole. Nobody lifted a finger against you." What can you say to that?' She rubs her neck. She still rolls those uneven cigarettes, thick in the middle and thin at the ends. 'I know everything now. There's also a man who had to collect the clothes of the people who were sent straight to the gas chambers on arrival. In the end he missed his turn. Do you ever think what it was like?'

'Yes.'

'And dreams? Do you dream about it? Do you see them in your dreams?'

'I often dream about my father. I am walking with him to a house which is at the end of a dark, slippery road. I have a feeling the road is covered with ice. When we are in front of the house it looks empty and abandoned. We go inside and walk through long corridors with doors on both sides. Each time we open a door we see a couple of people sitting there. Strange people. They don't look at us or at each other and they don't move. Each room is connected with another. None of them are empty. And yet the house gives the impression of being completely empty. Sometimes I see my father on an enormous plain. The ground is white and rugged. I stand at a distance looking at him and wait until he comes towards me. But then I see my sister approaching from the other side. They walk towards each other and go off together without noticing me.'

'Did you have a large family?'

'There were four of us.'

'No, I mean all your relatives.'

'Counting all my cousins and uncles and aunts there were more than sixty. I was able to check by the Red Cross letters.'

'I came to thirty-nine.'

'Was Aalten the only place you went into hiding?'

'No. First of all I was in the Veluwe for a few weeks, in a village teacher's cellar. There were five of us. It was cold and damp. There was a narrow passageway to the staircase from the cellar. The cellar door came out in the corridor. The teacher was afraid, we noticed that. We weren't allowed out and we had to keep deathly still. One morning, one of the five had hanged himself at the top of the cellar staircase. A boy of about twenty. He had done it while we were sleeping with the rope which had been tied round his own suitcase. When we discovered him he was already cold. I only looked at his feet. They turned very slowly half a circle and then back again. We couldn't stay there any more. I think they left him by the side of the road in a dry ditch the following evening. A boy with a round, childlike face.' She stubbed her cigarette-end into the ashtray and continued pressing on it. 'Everything goes on as before,' she muttered. 'You wonder sometimes how it's possible and you feel guilty.'

'Guilty?'

'Yes.'

'Why?'

'Because we're still here.'

'We've already discussed that.'

'Because we didn't do anything to stop them.'

'It was impossible.'

'Because we let them do anything they liked with us. That's why.'

'There's no point in going over it now.'

'You can't forget about it either, can you?'

'I try to.'

'After all, you've got Mark. That makes a difference.'

What was he coming for? What did he want with his separate room? First, see how the land lies and then carefully seek a reconciliation? Perhaps Tinka has already had enough of him or he of her and now I was back in favour.

I'd left my spot above the vines and climbed down the stony hill to the path behind the houses. The smoke from the smouldering rubbish wafted in my face. It was so pungent I had to close my eyes. I wouldn't go to the station. I'd let him arrive alone, let him ask the way. Let him walk to the Ponsaillers' with his suitcase, in vain. 'Madame left early this morning. She didn't say where she was going.'

I've already packed my suitcase but not closed it. The stove is out, the windows are thickly frosted over. I walk to and fro and check if I've forgotten anything. From the wall I take the posy of flowers that Mark gave me on my wedding day. It is dried up and faded. I blow on it and a cloud of dust rises.

'What are you doing?' I didn't hear her come in. She is wearing a camel-coloured duffle-coat and a woollen scarf on her head. Her nose is red. Her face has filled out, of late. Sometimes she puts make-up on. She looks at the bunch of flowers and from the flowers to the suitcase. 'Are you taking it with you?'

'Of course not.'

'Are you going to throw it away?'

'What else?'

'It's unlucky to throw it away.'

'I didn't know you were superstitious.'

'I'm not, but you are, aren't you?'

'I'll take the risk.' I shove the dried flowers in the stove, put a newspaper in and set it alight. It sputters briefly and there is a momentary noise as if everything is going through the chimney at once. 'It's gone just like that and you don't even smell it.'

'I have a cold, I can't smell anything.'

'Come south with me.'

'A good idea, but you're a bit late.'

'Would you have liked to come?'

'I've got other things to do.' She blows her nose and rubs her stiff cheeks.

'Are you so busy?'

'I'm doing all kinds of things. I'm cataloguing somebody's library. A man who had put his books in store somewhere and had them delivered to his home nice and neatly when he came out of hiding.'

'That happens too.'

She takes a couple of packets of cigarettes from her bag and throws them into the suitcase. 'Pinched from the office.'

She takes me to the station. We walk along Geldersekade, where the snow is so deep on the pavements that we have to walk in the road. Cars fling up brown mud. A couple of seagulls are standing stock-still on the ice in the canal from which pieces of rusty iron protrude. Perhaps it happened here. Or was it in

Groenburgwal after all, where her aunt lived? I have never pressed her further. Nor ever asked about the house. I want her to start talking about it herself. What do I know about her really? She talks to me only about the things she wants to forget, the war, the tribulations of being in hiding, the camps, an odd time about her youth and then mainly about her father. But when I'm sitting in her attic where she's always busy with something and see the things with which she's surrounded herself, her painting equipment, her books, her record-player with classical records, it's as if I'm meeting her for the first time. I suspect her of deliberately keeping me out of a world which restores life to normal for her.

She waits on the platform until the train starts moving. She walks along with it. I bend forward to give her a hand.

'Don't fall out,' she cries.

'Why should I do that?'

I close the window and put my luggage in the rack. The compartment is empty. I can sit where I like. I pick a corner seat. Once out from under the roof of the station, the white of the snow-covered embankments flashes through the window like a light.

'Madame, madame' I heard someone shout. Janine came running after me. 'Le train, madame, vite, vite!' She ran past me, her dark plaits flailing her back as if she was spurring herself on. Had she looked for me everywhere in the village? She didn't mind letting on that she was curious about mon mari. It was quite likely he would pretend that nothing had happened, that he would say nothing and had simply come for a holiday. I wouldn't ask him anything. Even if he were to say after a week that he had to go back.

A man with a straw hat came through the ticket-barrier, hand in hand with a small boy. The man took off his hat and waved to someone in the distance. Three women appeared with hampers, boxes and baskets. They waggled outside on each other's heels like ducks out of a cage. An old man with bow-legs. A nun in a grey habit. She was wearing spectacles with thin metal frames. Behind them came Mark, his head protruding above the nun's stiff head-dress. He was wearing a black winter overcoat.

'You look well.' He put down his suitcase and kissed me on my cheek. His face smelt of tobacco and a night without sleep in the train.

'Aren't you hot in that coat?'

'It was seven degrees below freezing when I left.' He took his coat off. 'You're right, it's warm here. Come to think of it, I noticed it in the train. It was easier to wear it.' He folded his coat with the lining outwards and put it over his arm.

'Won't it fit in your suitcase?'

'No, it's full.'

'Were you thinking of staying long?'

'Perhaps. If it's all right with you.'

It's all right with me. We have to go this way.'

The square was empty. No passengers had come out of the station after Mark. I pulled him by the arm to the side of the road in the shadow of the cypresses. We walked slowly. His suitcase banged against my leg and he put it in his other hand. While I looked at his face, the sharp creases round his mouth, the small, straight nose and his hair which was always long in the nape of his neck, a feeling came over me which I'd experienced before. A feeling that I had known him longer than those three years. Much longer than the day on which we first went to bed together, the evening when we sat reading by the light of candles which one of the boys had stolen from the Moses and Aaron Church. 'They smell of incense', Mark says, and he starts singing a Gregorian chant.

'I didn't know that you were a Catholic.'

'I'm lapsed, have been since I was fifteen. As a boy on Sundays I walked past the church more often than I went inside. But I'm not from a devout family. My mother was a believer, but my father hardly at all.'

'Did you go to confession?'

'Yes, that was part of it. But once I'd noticed that I didn't drop dead when I went to communion after concealing a sin, I began to see things differently. Fear disappeared. And fear keeps the sheep in the fold.'

'Perhaps it wasn't a sin.'

'Yes it was.'

'What had you done?'

'Been with girls in the woods.' He laughs. 'Dirty games. Taking their knickers off and feeling. They were very willing. I could have pleaded mitigating circumstances because I was provoked. I was about ten years old.'

'You began earlier than I did.'

'But you've caught up since.' Candles light his face from below. I see him briefly press his teeth into his bottom lip. It's a sign I understand, as if he's never been a stranger to me.

He did it again now.

'Shall I carry your coat?'

'No, it's fine like this.'

'You shouldn't have brought it.'

'I said – didn't I? – that it was cold. There's still

snow on the ground.'

'There's been snow here, too. When I arrived they told me they'd never had so much snow in years.'

'You wrote that in your letter.'

'Oh, you read it.'

'Why shouldn't I have read your letter?' He looks in front of him with raised eyebrows. 'You want to stay here, then?'

'For the time being, yes, I like it. I want to try and find something to do here. Pick grapes in the autumn, it pays well.'

'It'll be harder than you think.'

'That doesn't worry me. I also want to go to North Africa in a freighter.'

We agreed to meet at the pavement café La Marenda in Banyuls. Gilbert has to sort out a few affairs for his father who is a wine-grower. It surprises me that he does anything at all. He claims to have studied economics in Toulouse. I walk round the bay in the direction of Cap Doune past Aristide Maillol's house in an overgrown garden. There is a bronze figure of a woman between two eucalyptus trees. Her breasts and stomach are golden, as if they are regularly polished. The sky above the sea is dark. It is getting colder. The tramontana's beginning to blow. I go back into the wind which is tugging at the crowns of the palms, causing shutters to clatter and blowing a flurry of foam across the pebbled beach. La Marenda's hanging sign swings creaking to and fro. A waiter takes in the table-cloths from the tables outside. I look across the empty promenade from behind one of the windows.

'The man you were talking to yesterday in Frontaulé – he sails to Algiers, doesn't he?'

'You mean Antoine?'

'I don't know what he's called.'

'Antoine Sagols.'

'Does he take passengers?'

'Why? Do you want to go to the other side?'

'Yes, I want to go to Algiers. In a while.'

There are red veins in the marble top, one of which disappears under Gilbert's notebook. He is doing some calculations with a pencil be borrowed from the waiter. The blue sweater he is wearing makes his tanned skin seem slightly purple. It might just be a trick of the light. He continues his calculations, tense, as if it doesn't add up.

'You've got quite a few plans, haven't you? Were you also contemplating coming back some time?'

He puts down his suitcase and puts his coat over it. We were high up. To the left there was part of the bay and the lighthouses; in the distance to the right, the bare foothills of the Pyrenees.

'That too.' I point to the asphalt path which went up high behind the bay, into the hills. 'That's the way to Port-Vendres.'

'Have you been there yet?' He rubs his handkerchief over his face.

'I go there regularly. You can walk it. It's a nice path. There's also a bus.'

'Is it like this place?'

'No, it's a small harbour. I once walked back one evening after I'd drunk a whole bottle of wine.'

'Did you drink it all on your own?'

'With friends.'

'You've got friends here already.'
'Yes.'

The tramontana is still blowing. It's past ten when we are standing on the dark promenade, wet from the flying foam. The sea batters the white hulls of the fishermen's boats high on the beach. I've said that I shall go back alone. We've spent the whole evening in La Marenda with friends of Gilbert, the majority Catalan. I understand only a tenth of what is said. They drink pastis and, because I don't like it, Gilbert has ordered a bottle of wine for me. He tries to explain the jokes which are being told. I miss most of the punch lines because of the constant laughter. I get fed up with it, it tires me, I might just as well be part of the furniture, although the women in the company constantly laugh across at me, which I don't like either. Perhaps it's the wine making me uppity. When we get outside my head is throbbing and there's a weight pressing on my stomach. I want to run away fast.

'I'm not going to let you go alone. The last bus doesn't go any further than Port-Vendres.'

'Then I'll walk the rest.'

'The road isn't lit.'

'I can find it with my eyes closed.'

'But the tramontana . . .'

'I come from a country where the wind never stops blowing.'

'I'll go with you.'

'No, Gilbert. Let me go.'

'Stay here.'

'No.'

'OK, then I'll have someone else tonight.'

'Merde.' I knock his hand away which is pressing on my upper arm and turn round.

'Sepha, petite sotte!' He yells it at me as I set off running into the dark, an immense void of wind, of gusts which pull at my jacket, whip my hair in front of my face, spatter sea water against my legs.

'Shall we go on?' Mark picked up his suitcase. He looked like the first tourist of the season, out of his element in his black Dutch shoes and his black coat. 'I can well imagine that you don't want to go back.' He came and walked close beside me.

'You don't need much here, you can live cheaply.'

'You look well.'

'You've said that already.'

'I'm saying it again, if I may. You've never looked as well. I've never known you like that.'

'No? Well, that's one advantage then.'

'Is it far?'

'Can you see that white house? That's it.'

I pointed out the Ponsaillers' house to him. It was taller than the other houses in this part of the village. The mimosa tree formed a soft yellow patch in front of the green-railed balcony. I saw Janine pop outside and immediately run in again. She went in to say that I was coming. I hadn't bothered to tell him that everyone was aware he was coming, that he had already been expected even before he'd planned to come. They knew him, they knew the reason he'd come. They knew more than I did. I went through the garden gate first. There was nobody to be seen. They were looking at us from the kitchen window, we couldn't get out of it. The outer door was open and then came Madame Ponsailler's voice: 'Madame Courtis, Madame Hollet, venez, le voilà, le jeune mari, le voilà. . . .'

They jostled each other in the doorway to the kitchen, staring over each other's shoulders, came into the corridor, the members of the family in front of us, the neighbours behind us, and Mark, clearly nonplussed, shook hands and gave one-syllable answers to the questions about his journey, whether he'd been able to sleep in the train, how he thought I looked and what he thought of the country – pays pittoresque et plaisant, pays de lumière, de soleil et de joie, I knew the eulogies by heart, they weren't an exaggeration and we nodded and walked upstairs, felt them push us upstairs with their eyes till we reached the dark doorway where we bumped into each other and I looked for the door handle.

The room was cool and twilit. The blinds had been let down. There were striped shadows on the dark brown oilcloth. Someone had tidied up. The basket with shopping was on the table.

'This is my room.' I raised the blind and gestured. The wash-stand of marbled wood with the jug, the basin, the faded prints on the moss-green wallpaper, the two chairs, the big bed with the crocheted bedspread, the mirror-fronted wardrobe, the portrait of old Monsieur Ponsailler, the lamp with the red silk tasselled cloth over it. 'Mine,' I said, and flicked the tassels so that he could hear that there were little bells in them.

'Crazy,' Mark said. He had taken his jacket off. 'Little bells on a lamp. Who thought that up?'

'I can't imagine it was the Ponsaillers. Perhaps somebody who stayed here. What do you think of it otherwise?'

'A nice room.'

'Yes.' It was unique at that moment. I felt as if we were together in a room for the first time. I hung his winter coat in the cupboard. I was glad not to see it any more. It had irritated me from the start. I combed my hair in front of the small mirror above the wash-stand. I put my hands into the lukewarm water in the jug and wet my face.

'Do you want to freshen up?' I thought he was standing behind me. The water ran down the opening in the neck of my dress to my stomach. I shivered a little and felt for the towel with my eyes closed.

He was leaning over the balcony, smoking. I went and stood next to him and pointed to the closed door to the right. 'The other room is next door.'

He kept staring in front of him. 'I once went on a cycling trip with a friend to the Ardennes. We took a tent. It rained four days non-stop. On the fifth day we woke up to the sun, which shone through a crack in the sailcloth. We crawled out of the tent and climbed a hill which we'd been looking at all the previous days. When we were at the top we saw undulating countryside, woods, small castles and a river with rapids. We thumped each other and started to yell, steam rose from our damp clothing and we ran down the hill, into the wet grass of the meadow, delirious from our discovery.'

'Do you want to see the room?' I led him over the balcony and pushed the door open. The stale air of an unused room. There was a vase with mimosa, apparently put there by Janine.

'A completely different room – smaller.'

'For one person.'

'You could have had this room, too.'

'I didn't, though. You wanted a separate room, that's what you wrote.'

'Yes.'

'You can work here quietly if you want.'

'That's the idea.'

'Have you a permanent job with the newspaper now?'

'As good as. I have an assignment to write a series of articles.'

'You said that you didn't want to take any advance.'

'I decided I could now.'

'Why the change?'

'Can't you understand that?'

'No, I can't understand it.'

'I was curious about you. How you were spending your time.'

'Oh yes?'

'Whether you were alone.'

'Who did you think I'd be with?'

'Someone you'd met.'

'And you wouldn't like that.'

'I suspected something when you said you had friends here.'

'Do you want to be my chaperone or something?'

'If it's inconvenient . . . you must say so.'

'That's a fine start. Did you want to accuse me of something?'

Opposite each other with the bed in between us, the bedspread completely smooth. My knees rubbed against the wooden side.

My parents' bedstead with plump cushions supported

by a bolster. If I thump it, a dent appears which stays there. I pull the bedspread straight and go to the wash-basin, turn on the tap and take off my pyjamas. I open the door a crack and listen. I hear nothing. I'm by myself upstairs. I quietly close the door and turn the key. I stand in front of the big mirror of the linen cupboard and pass my hands over my breasts, feeling the stiffness of my nipples against the palms of my hands. 'It's time you start wearing a brassière,' my mother says. She has already bought one for me but it's too big and I don't wear it. I open the linen cupboard and take a shawl from the bottom shelf, hold it in front of me, let it gradually drop to my waist, bend forwards so that my breasts seem bigger, look at myself sideways. I wrap the shawl around my stomach, lay my hand over my pubic hair and come closer to the mirror. My face is burning. I have goose-pimples.

'Do you want one?' He held out his packet of cigarettes and I took one. A cigarette means respite. You can put something off, look for a way out. He gave me a light across the bed. A spark fell on the bedspread, a black dot. He looked at me, one eye shut because of the smoke. 'Your neck is brown.'

'Of course. I'm in the sun here every day.'

'You seem different to me.'

'I'm not different. Perhaps you don't know me well enough.'

'I thought about that in Amsterdam. I imagined how you were.'

'Did you have time for that?'

'I wondered what you were doing. I wanted to see

you, I wanted to talk to you.'

'We've talked so much already. It never got us anywhere.'

'I know, but now it's different.' It seemed one only ever had platitudes for conversations like this. They were predictable from one minute to the next.

'Different for you.'

'For you too, I think. Let's go next door.'

We walked across the balcony. A corridor of warm air. I let down the blind. Mark put his suitcase against the wall, took off his shoes and sat down on the bed.

'What are you doing?' Gilbert asks.

I put the red cape which is lying under my dress over my shoulders. I'm standing at the foot end, he's sitting at the head and pours wine into the glasses which the landlady has put on the bedside cupboard. He keeps my glass so that I have to go towards him to get it. 'Qu'est-que tu fais? Jouer à cache-cache, non?' He laughs and pulls the cape from my shoulders.

I pause before I drink. I should like to postpone everything, just stay sitting there with the glass in my hand on the edge of the bed in the hotel room where only the light above the wash-stand is burning. But Gilbert grabs my glass and lays me on my back.

'It looks as if your breasts are brown as well.' A game, but it still affected me, the way he looked at me, the way I knew.

'They are.'

'Where can you sunbathe in the nude here?'

'On the balcony, with a sheet over the railings. And

there are a lot of tiny beaches in between the rocks. You have to know where they are.'

He pushed his shoes away with his foot and nodded a couple of times without looking up, his eyebrows frowning as if he were contemplating all kinds of peeping Toms who spied on me daily from behind rocks. I felt like undressing when I saw his face darken, tense and greedy. But I waited.

'It's brown all over.'

'All over?'

'Yes, all over, look.' And I undressed. I threw my clothes on the floor, stood in front of him with my arms raised and slowly turned round.

'See.'

He sprang up and his eyes went all over my body. He lifted my breasts one at a time. His hands went over my back and my thighs and the tops of his fingers stroked the insides. He kissed me there.

'Your skin is beautiful. You put me to shame.'

'Let me look.'

I had to laugh at his snow-white body which he pressed against mine.

I'll have to tell him, I think, before he notices himself. He must know. I kick my pyjama bottoms, which are at the foot of the bed, into a ball. My toes are briefly caught up in the elastic. He's leaning on his elbow and trying to pick out my face in the dark. The candle next to the bed is finished. I keep my arms crossed over my stomach, my left foot touches his thigh-bone.

'I've never . . .'

He laughs and strokes my leg, lets his hand rest on my knee.

'You didn't give the impression . . . I thought . . .'

'I know what you thought, when I said I wanted to go to bed with you.'

'If you want us . . .'

'No, Mark, I want to now.'

The sky is a little lighter than the houses which stand beyond the window like a vaguely sketched piece of scenery. There's a rhythmical zoom of aircraft overhead. I ought not to be hearing it. Not now. I pull him towards me and automatically open my legs. His movements are cautious. The pain I feel quickly lessens.

My stretched-out feet pressed against the bottom of the bed. The strips of light from the moving blind quivered. We smoked a cigarette, and because the ashtray was on the floor he had to keep bending over me and we started again. We drank wine from the same glass in the shadow of the mimosa from the balcony. Perhaps there was another one in the other room, but I didn't bother.

A boy with a goat on a rope came past. Now and again he hit the animal on its flanks. To the left of the hills there was a grey-blue strip of sea or sky, you couldn't tell the difference, and in front of it was the village in a basin of warmth, every tree, every house sharply defined against the dark, bare slopes in the background. Mark continued to look, while he gave me the glass.

'Looking at this I have to admit you're right.'

'You forget everything here. It just happens.'

'What did you do yesterday?'

'Yesterday? I walked to Port-Vendres.'

'Yesterday, no, the day before yesterday, Sunday, I

was messing about in the kitchen with the gas stove.'

'You'll have to get the thing repaired.'

'Yes, but it gave off some heat at any rate. It thawed out the kitchen window. Were you in Port-Vendres?'

'On the way I met a man with a donkey. He asked me if I knew the time.'

'Did you know him?'

'No. I didn't know the time exactly either. I thought it was about three o'clock.' I filled the glass. There was not much left in the bottle.

'Nice wine.'

'Just vin ordinaire. You'll be able to taste the difference if you drink Banyuls, the wine of the region.'

'Have you drunk it often?'

'A couple of times.'

'By yourself?'

'It's not wine you drink alone.' Two girls were being chased along the path by two boys in blue overalls. They disappeared round the corner, yelling. 'How long do you want to stay here?'

'I don't know yet, it depends.'

'On what?'

'Oh. . . .' He made a gesture as if throwing something over the balcony. He looked down and his hair fell forward. He ran his fingers through it. 'It wasn't so easy to get away.'

'Did you manage to get a good exchange rate for your money?'

He nodded. 'Very good, in fact. Tinka knew somebody in a bank, a cousin. He also tipped me off how I should take the money across the border. Simply in a folded newspaper. No problem. French Customs did catch a Belgian who was sitting opposite me. He'd taken his francs from his pocket and put them in his shoe. And my coat was hanging next to me with the newspaper half sticking out. All I needed to do was to show them my wallet.'

The empty wine bottle had rolled across the balcony and come to rest on the cement floor between the railings. We both looked at it. He'd been here a couple of hours now. All that time I'd been waiting for him to mention her name. I had even more or less asked for it. But now that it had been mentioned, it was like a piece of plaster suddenly falling from the ceiling and I didn't know quite how to react. Mark leant over the railings again. His shirt was creased. He had ironed it himself and missed the back.

'Didn't she want to come?'

'She's never been south.' He came and sat next to me, picked up the glass from the floor and let it roll between his hands.

'No?'

'She liked the idea.'

'I'll go and get another bottle of wine.'

'She came with me.'

'Came with you?'

'To Paris. She had to be in Paris.'

'Do you know that here they think Holland is just above Paris? They think Paris is a long way away. The majority of the people have never been there.'

'It's true. It's an endless journey.'

'You came on the wrong train. I ought to have written to tell you. You should have taken the Barcelona Express. It's faster. It leaves Paris in the morning and arrives here in the evening.'

'I heard that later.'

'Is she coming later?'

'Well, perhaps in a week.'

'A week?'

'She had some things to do in Paris. She was going to call by after she'd finished there.'

'Really?'

'Yes. She said something like that.'

'And you, did you think she should?'

'No. I wanted to come here alone.' He stood up and took a few steps across the balcony. 'I told her that I would go alone. Of course I didn't think for a minute she would come with me. She was in the train. She didn't come into my compartment until we'd passed Haarlem.'

'Nice surprise.'

'I'll write to tell her that she shouldn't come. I'd decided to do that in any case on the way.'

'You should have told her.'

'Yes, yes, I ought to have done, of course. But I thought perhaps she won't come. Perhaps it's just a threat.' He rubbed his forehead vigorously.

'Do you know her address in Paris?'

'Yes.'

'She'll probably come anyway.' More than half of the balcony was in shadow now. I picked up the empty bottle. 'I'm going to get some wine. I'll be back in a minute.'

Madame Ponsailler was in the kitchen with a basket of beans on her knee. Her visitors had gone. She stood up and said something I didn't understand. Taking a chance, I replied that everything was fine and saw to it that I got out of the house waving the bottle. A drop fell on to my skirt. A tiny drop of blood.

The girl pulls me under the roof of the cycle shed in

the playground. She lifts her dress up. The blood is on her slip. She's older than I am and quite a bit bigger. She bends towards me. 'Have you seen it?' she whispers. I look at her face and from her face to her skirt. There's blood on her clothes and she laughs. 'I've started my periods,' she says. 'You haven't, have you?' I shake my head. 'But your sister has, of course.'

She stays standing there with the hem of her dress in her hands. She has a couple of pimples on her forehead. Her hair almost touches my face. I move a little backwards and feel the sharp edge of a rear light in the back of my knee. '"It's nothing to worry about,"' my mother said. '"Ellen simply has a little tummy upset."'

She pushes me aside in the hallway and goes upstairs hurriedly with my sister. She locks the bedroom door. I can hear her walking to and fro and talking in a hushed voice; the door of the linen cupboard creaks, there's a drumming noise in the water-pipes. I pretend to the girl that I know everything.

The woman from the épicerie had black eyes with dark rings round them, heavy eyelashes and hair on her upper lip. She asked how le mari was getting on. I said that everything was going well and gave her the empty bottle. She puts a full one on the counter in front of me, a greasy, brown surface covered with holes and scratches. She could imagine how I felt, she said. Such a long time without le mari wasn't much fun. I agreed. As I pulled the shop door to, she was still nodding at me.

At the corner I realized that I'd walked the length of the street instead of going back. I stood still. In five minutes I could be back in the room. We had only a week. And then? What would he do? He might just as well have gone somewhere else; to Argelès, for example, a few kilometres further up from Collioure. I needn't have known. Perhaps we would have met each other then by accident in a pavement café in Perpignan. You here too? This is Gilbert. I met him when I came here. We celebrated carnival together, we climb together, swim and lie in the sun, eat and drink together, go to bed together without expecting anything of each other.

The square reeked of fish. Men and women stood at long tables sorting the catch in the fish hall on the corner, a dusky room with arched windows. Their blue aprons glistened. I went down the steep street towards the beach. Close to the water there was a row of fishing-boats in which small boys were playing. Next to them in the shadow of the steep cliff sat the net repairers, old women all in black. The noise they made as I went by was something in between praying and singing. I walked up the steps hollowed out of the rock to a kind of terrace surrounded by a parapet of rough stones, and with my back to the sea I looked for the white house with the balcony. From there it was just visible. Perhaps he was standing looking at me. But I should only be able to see him if he walked to the other corner. The mimosa tree concealed the door of my room.

But to the right, and much higher, was the ruin I had been to with Gilbert the day before. Nobody goes there in the off season, he says. We'd eaten in Port-Vendres and come back with the bus. A woman turns round and asks him how his father is. They speak in Catalan. We get out at the bend before Collioure. I feel as if my dress will have to be taken off me like a plaster as Gilbert pulls me up the path which is strewn with loose stones and practically impassable. We lie on the hard grass behind a wall with alcoves more than half a metre deep. If I put my head round the wall I can see the dark coastline up to Banyuls, the smooth sea on which yachts are cruising, the Sunday bathers, the green and reddy-brown of the slopes. There is no wind, no noise. I've never done it in the open air before. I keep my eyes open. It's as if the sky whirls over me in spirals, rushing; it makes me dizzy. I dig my nails into his back, on which the shadow of the wall falls. I get tired, but he doesn't let up. He takes what he can. I think, I wish I was here alone.

The bottle became heavy in my hand. I'd not thought of putting it on the ground. I stood up. The old fishermen who had their permanent rendezvous here said good-day to me. I took the shortest way back, across the beach, across the square, past the post office. The chickens in the front garden scampered away as if I was a stranger.

'I thought you just went to get some wine?' Mark lay on the bed. Next to him on the floor there was an ashtray full of cigarette-ends.

'I did.' I put the bottle on the table, inserted the corkscrew and pulled the cork out cleanly.

'Is it so far away?'

'No. I'll make something to eat. I've got pâté.'

I took the French bread, pâté and the butter from the basket. I pushed the table near to the bed and sat next to him. While we ate and drank in turns he told me that he could get a permanent job at the paper in a few months' time, in the foreign editors' section. 'I like the idea. What do you think?'

'If you like the idea, you should do it.'

'I've also thought about finishing university. After all, I've done my preliminaries.'

'Why did you go and study law in the first place?'

'I had to choose something.'

'And then it's always law.'

'Well, my father would rather I had done medicine, but it didn't appeal to me. Can you see me as a pill?'

'No.' I had to laugh.

'And you, what have you done?'

'When?'

'Here, I mean.'

'Me? Nothing. Lain on my back.'

'It's done you good, in any event. Do you want to go back with me?'

'Yes, of course.'

'In a couple of weeks?'

'Right.'

'I've already written to tell her not to come.'

I was sitting with a piece of bread in my hand and looking at the pâté. It was a greyish brown. There were also dark pieces in it, a black triangle in the middle, shining like liquorice.

'Why did you agree to meet her here?'

'That was her idea, I've already told you.'

'But if you didn't want to . . .'

'She knew what I thought. Recently, I've come to see everything in a different light.'

He had already said that it was different, that I was different and now he thought differently. I leant against his knees which were pulled up. Both of us had started talking more quietly as if somebody was listening to us.

'But do you think it will be different?'

'We can try, at any rate.'

I did not reply.

'Sepha?' His hand passed slowly over my back.

'Yes.'

I felt lethargic, my eyelids were heavy. I heard him talk but his voice became softer and softer, further and further away. I had difficulty following him and I nodded to show that I was listening. As I stretched out my legs I noticed that he was no longer sitting on the bed. He was unpacking his suitcase. I heard him put his shaving equipment on the wash-stand, open the cupboard door and hang his clothes up. I ask him what we should do with the other room. Come with me to the other room, I say. But we cannot get the door open. After a struggle we succeed. In the room there are a lot of people crowding round the bed in which someone is apparently lying. They whisper; it sounds like hissing. I try to work my way to the front. A bottle of wine is broken against the sides of the bedstead. What lovely blood, a woman cries. I'm now standing in front of the bed. There's an old man lying on it with a white moustache. His eyes are closed, his face is yellow. Monsieur Ponsailler is holding his arm tight. He hasn't got his Basque hat on and I can see that he has got curly black hair. This is him, he says. I want to move backwards but I can't get away. If I look down at the floor I see that I am standing in a red, sticky substance. The soles of my shoes are stuck fast in it. Somebody tries to pull me out by tugging at my shoulder. 'Wake up. Wake up.'

Mark stood bent over me. He had put on another shirt. 'Let's go into the village and eat, I feel like something tasty.'

It was dark when we came out of the restaurant. We'd been there a long time. All around us people had eaten loudly and drunk freely. It was as if Mark unwound for the first time. His face was red from the sun and the wine. He talked excitedly, clinked glasses with people at the table next to us, paid me compliments all the time and stroked my thigh under the table. As we went outside he put his arm round me.

Music was coming from the fish hall. The trestles and barrels had been put to one side. Girls with long, black hair, fat girls in tight jumpers danced with each other on the cement floor which had been swilled clean. The boys stood round silently, smoking nonchalantly. We went down to the beach and walked in the direction of the lighthouse at the end of the pier, carefully stepping over the rocks. A wind had got up. You could smell the salt water crashing up against the breakwater.

'Here are the stairs.' I took his hand.

Blinded by the stream of light which hit us, we climbed up and, feeling our way, found the rail. A train whistled in the distance.

'The Barcelona Express.'

'Is it only just arriving? I'm glad actually that I took the night train. When it gets light you suddenly see that you're in the South. And you see the village lying there as you come out of the tunnel. When we came into the station I saw you standing there. First of all I thought you were a local girl.'

I said that I felt the same too, that I sometimes felt that I'd always lived here. I loved the village, I loved the people who accepted me and made me feel as though I belonged there. I stood on the little beach among the fishermen's wives waving the boats off. I went along on the sardine-catching trips. When they had come in I helped to carry the baskets. I stood talking in the shop about the scarcity of food, the damage to the harvest and saying that everything was so expensive. I handed in my ration coupons for matière grasse and American tinned meat and lived like the rest did on nouilles and grilled fish, bread and wine and fruit. I belonged here. By a lucky chance I had been transplanted and my roots had taken.

'But you said that you wanted to go back.'

I bent further over the railing and saw in the flashes of light his protruding head and flapping hair. I wanted to go back, I wanted to stay here, I wanted to go with Sagols's orange boat to Algiers. I didn't know.

'Come on, it's getting cold.' Again he put his arm around me.

Behind us the sea rolled between the rocks. In front of us lay the village, full of tiny spots of light, a night sky which had dropped between the slopes. Guitar music came from a house, a girl sang and men's laughter came from the open door of the Café des Sports. We walked quicker, holding each other's hands. We felt the path rising, our breathing becoming quicker. A dog whined, stifled, as if somebody was keeping its mouth shut. You could hear the rustle of animals creeping away in the bushes.

There was somebody standing at the fence. She stood with her back towards us, suitcases and bags around her. I recognized her blonde hair. We stopped in our tracks simultaneously. Mark let go of my hand. I whispered: 'The Barcelona Express.'

She turned round. 'Hello, are you there? I've walked all the way from the station with my luggage. Apparently you can't get taxis here.'

'There aren't any taxis here,' I said.

'I thought you would be coming in a week.'

'It was a dead loss in Paris. And I felt like going south. I thought, why should I stay here in the cold? I took the express early this morning.'

A strip of light glowed behind the kitchen window. I'll say that it's my sister and that I suddenly have to return to Amsterdam. I've made up so much, a bit more won't make any difference.

'I'll take you to the hotel.' Mark picked up one of the suitcases.

'You've got rooms here, haven't you?'

'It's better if you go to the hotel.' He picked up another bag, turned towards me briefly. 'I shan't be long.'

'A pity you can't stay here,' I said. I pushed the gate open. Without turning round, I went inside and walked tiptoe past the kitchen door.

The lamp in my room gave off a rosy glow. I pulled the bedspread straight and hung up the dress which I'd worn that afternoon in the cupboard. I pushed Mark's winter coat to the back; the hanger scraped over the rail. His shoes were under the wash-stand, neatly together. I pushed my foot between them so that the heels were apart, folded the bedspread and hung it over the foot of the bed. I drank some water. I combed my hair with Mark's comb while I looked at the prints on the wall: a bowl of flowers, faded, a church, faded too, both in a brown frame. I kicked off my shoes and lay on the bed but stood up again, undressed and crawled between the sheets. All I could hear was the blinds tapping against the window-frame. Otherwise it was quiet.

But I could hear something outside. The crunch

105

of cinders. Someone approached. Someone walked hurriedly along the path. The gate shut. Quick footsteps on the gravel. In the corridor, up the stairs. I recognized his footsteps.

Friday, 21st April 1950

I was standing in the hall putting on my coat when the telephone rang. I went inside and picked it up. It was Yona. Her voice sounded agitated.

'Are you home? I'm just going to pop in. I'll be there in a quarter of an hour.'

'What's the matter, what is it?'

In reply I got a long engaged tone. I put the receiver down. I had wanted to say that I was on the point of leaving. But she hadn't given me a chance. I was annoyed that I hadn't reacted at once, that I'd been thwarted from doing what I'd planned by a few words. After I'd hung my coat on the peg I went inside again. I had got up with Mark. We had had coffee and fried eggs for breakfast. I promise him that I shall go to the house. They're coming today to switch on the gas and electricity. He gives me the keys.

'Make sure you're there at ten. I can't get away.'

I'm sitting with the keys in my hand, letting them knock against each other. They're on a piece of string. One is made of black metal, the other copper coloured with a number on it.

'The biggest is for the outside door, the other for the door to the flat,' Mark says. He points to it with his arm above the bread-basket. 'It's dead simple. You don't have to examine them like that.'

'I'm not. They're quite ordinary keys.'

'Yes. And it's a nice flat.' He stands up and buttons up his coat. 'You ought to be glad.'

Glad, perhaps. Sometimes I try to imagine that this is my first house, that I started my life here that evening in '44. But there's no point. Right away I see another house with a wide vestibule and glass doors to stop draughts which one day I fall through. I have a deep cut in my wrist which needs stitching. Six stitches. I still have a scar. There's a round landing on the staircase on which we play tag with chairs from the bedroom as trees. A few houses along from us on the corner there's a flower shop which I go to with my sister. 'Keep tight hold of her,' my mother says. There's a heavy, sweet smell in the shop which gives me an oppressive feeling in my head. But it also comes from the florist's hand. His fingers catch in my hair. And then there's the hand of my grandfather who is staying with us and utters a prayer above my head. On Saturdays we have to remember not to touch the light switches, not to pick up paper and pencil, not to light matches, not to put the milk near the meat. He says: 'You're like your grandmother.' I look in the mirror and have difficulty seeing myself with white hair, a false plait at the back of my head, in a black dress with a diamond brooch. I'm called after her. I can't see any similarity.

After Mark leaves I remain at the breakfast table playing with the keys to the house which I've not yet seen. What should I do? It's empty, with cold windows, bare walls, creaking floors. I've no connection with it whatsoever. Going to live in another house is distancing yourself from something, starting again and adding reminiscences to earlier ones so that the earlier ones are even further away.

It's raining. I had gone to sit on the window-sill to wait for Yona. The rain made circles in the water of the canal. I started counting the windows in the building on the other side. I'd done it before but I wasn't certain exactly how many there were. Tapping my finger against the pane I came to eighty-three – seventeen attic windows and sixty-six big windows in three rows of twenty-two. Afterwards I started on the towers, but I was put off by a fat woman who stopped in front of the building. She took a green shawl out of her errand-basket, shook it out violently as if she'd dusted something with it. Then she tried to put it over her head. She didn't manage it because of the wind. She put her bag on the window-sill, flung back her head so that the rain struck her face.

'There's crazy Germaine,' Gilbert says. She's wearing a red swimming-costume and her enormous body bulges out on all sides. She comes giggling from behind the rocks. While she stumbles over the pebbles to the sea, she loses her balance. She shrieks. She covers the last part on hands and knees. When the sea is up to her knees she bends forward, passes something through the water and holds it with outstretched arms above her face which is thrown right back. She laughs, her tongue sticking out of her mouth.

'What's she doing?'

'She has a tube which she lets the sea run through.' He lies outstretched, his legs apart. A silver coin on a chain glistens among the hair on his chest. Germaine pulls the tube a few more times through the water and moves in our direction. Her thighs wobble against each other. Gilbert lies immobile. Only his chest rises and falls imperceptibly as if he's trying to hold his breath. 'We've got visitors,' I say softly.

'Pretend you're asleep, otherwise we'll have her on our hands all morning.'

It hadn't been difficult to part from him. He'd started making too many demands of me. Mark had arrived just in time. I run across him a couple of times in Port-Vendres, in Banyuls, and we greet each other like people who have fleetingly known each other. That's how it should always be. And that's the way it is when I'm sitting with Mark one morning in the Café des Sports, opposite Château Collioure. He wants to know who the man is who walks past and I wave to. Gilbert lifts his hand, nods and turns round again.

'Was there something between you?'

'What on earth makes you think that?'

'Of course there was. He looks attractive. And a woman alone here. . . .' He follows Gilbert with his eyes as if he thinks he can discover something to confirm it in his back. I wonder whether he now makes a mental leap to Tinka and the randy men in Cannes. She left here the day after she arrived. I didn't see her again. She sent a coloured postcard of a white hotel in a garden full of palms with greetings to us both.

'Sporting of her.'

'Oh, she's very generous,' Mark says. He picks up the card again and studies it closely. 'So she's staying there.'

'Wouldn't you rather have gone with her? She does things more lavishly.'

'I'm fine here.'

The fat woman had passed by. A boy wearing black wellingtons jumped in a pool. The water splashed over the pavement. He came back again and stamped one foot in the water. He seemed to be satisfied because he moved on.

At first after we returned from the South it seems as if we have brought with us the atmosphere in which we had lived there. But it doesn't take long. Now it's Mark's work with the paper that makes him come home so irregularly. He also works night-shifts.

'You must do something,' he says. 'Try something.'

'What? I wouldn't know what, I can't do anything.'

Nevertheless, I think about doing something myself. I look at advertisements, note addresses wanting models. Ladies with a lot of spare time can earn attractive pin-money. I learn from the clothing factory I go to that my measurements aren't right and I forget about the pin-money. I haven't a vocation for demonstrating coffee-machines. That winter my tonsillitis comes back and I lie in bed with a high temperature. In Collioure it was over in a few days; here it takes weeks. Mark is irritated if I'm ill; he stays in town longer, and sometimes comes home late at night. He knows that Yona looks after me. Shortly after our return she talks derisorily about our ideal marriage. Now she says nothing, but I can see from her face what she thinks.

It's still raining. I look at the dripping trees. I would miss the trees and the water. Wherever I went I had to look outside first. Sometimes a view can compensate for the inside.

In Thomas's studio there are no windows; there is only a glass roof. I meet him in a place near Nieuwmarkt where short films are shown. We sit on low benches which are close together. Somebody behind me doesn't know what to do with his legs, his knees perpetually bump into my back. I move forward a little and bump into a man in a dark-blue knitted sweater. He turns round, asks whether he's in the way, whether I can see. He has a long face with narrow eyes below a high forehead and a wide moustache, darker than his hair. He proposes that we change places. While we step over the bench, the lights go out. I hold on to him briefly, our legs stroke each other. Later he takes me home. He says that he's a painter. I promise him that I'll come and have a look at his studio sometime.

The glass roof is a new sensation to me at first. I feel as if I'm lying in a cabin. When I come in he immediately puts down his brushes. Apparently he paints only from a sense of duty; he can stop just like that. 'Carry on,' I say. He doesn't realize that I like watching somebody doing something, someone engrossed in their work but who knows I'm there. Looking at his back, wondering who knitted his jumper, inhaling the smell of paint, thumbing through a magazine, stroking the grey cat. But he always wants to immediately, he doesn't even allow me time to get in the mood. And then there are the children. I hear them scampering over the rafters. They squeeze through the skylight, creep on their stomachs to the edge of the glass and press their noses to the window.

'Where do the children come from?'

'The neighbours.'

'Don't you do anything about them?'

'They can't see anything through frosted glass.'

'Why do they look, then?'

'Oh, leave them alone. They've been doing it for so long.'

I turned away from the window. The quarter of an hour was up. Just like Yona to come much too late, to be secretive about things which are unimportant.

'She's somebody who comes with instructions for use,' Mark once said.

'If you forget to keep to them, you tread on all the sore spots.'

'That's why they don't heal, because nobody makes allowances.'

Her face was white, she had dark rings round her eyes. Her wet hair fell in rats' tails over her head. I hung her raincoat in the kitchen on the hook above the sink. When I went in she was in the middle of the room polishing her glasses. I pushed her in a chair and sat opposite her. I looked at my nails, pulled a thread from my skirt, smoothed down my nylons. We once had a couple visiting us, and the husband had something to discuss with Mark. The woman took her nail-file out of her bag after about five minutes and began to do her nails. When her husband stood up, she brushed down her skirt and said: 'Well, that's that done.' Those were the first words she spoke.

Yona sat bent forward, her glasses in her hand. She was swinging them, holding them by one earpiece. A droplet from her hair fell next to her shoe. I asked her if anything had happened. She shook her head. 'Nothing's happened, there's nothing.' She paused. 'I can't go on.'

I knew the routine. I would now be told how everyone, the entire world, was against her, and I said: 'I thought it had been going rather well recently with your work.'

She shrugged her shoulders. 'I've practically nothing to do any more.'

'Why's that?'

'It's no good. It's so damned mediocre, what I do.'

'But you had various assignments.'

'I've dropped them, I'm giving it up.'

'What are you going to do?'

'Nothing. It's all so pointless.' She curled up, supporting her head in her hands. I could hardly hear her when she said: 'He's come back.' I didn't realize at first whom she was talking about, I was taken aback by the words 'come back'. It can happen that somebody comes back after five years. Sometimes I imagine it. I recognize the stance of somebody on the tram, the gait of somebody coming out of the station. Somebody crosses a square and I have to follow him for streets and streets because I'm not certain – until I discover that I've made a mistake again, and have to admit that I'm playing a game with myself.

'Who?' I ask. 'Who's come back?'

She sat up straight. 'No, come on, don't be daft. You couldn't think that.'

'No.'

'I mean . . . that friend I had who went to America

before the war.'

'Is he here?'

'On holiday, you know, doing Europe in three weeks.'

'Did you meet him?'

She nodded. She put her glasses on the table and stared at her hands in her lap. Her fingers were clasped together; her knuckles stuck out as if they were white knobs which had been put on separately. 'I kept thinking about him all those years.' Her mouth barely moved. She didn't look up. She talked as if she was alone. It doesn't matter, nobody's listening, nobody's looking. 'You'll probably think it's ridiculous again, but for me it was something. I could think about him in a different way from the others – he was alive.'

'Did you write to each other?'

'Not for long. He wrote to me after he had asked about me at the Red Cross. They were able to give him my address instead of the name of a camp and a date. I wrote back. I've not heard anything for the last two years.'

'Didn't he let you know he was coming?'

'No. Suddenly he was there.' She drew her hands apart. 'At first I didn't recognize him. He's become an American businessman, a bit on the fat side, with sunglasses.'

'What do you expect? A person changes in ten years. He was still a boy when he left.'

'I know that, but. . . .' She looked outside, her eyes blinking, her lips clamped together.

In three years I should be thirty. What had I done, what would I do that was of any significance which would show there was a point to our being here while the others weren't? My Uncle Max's twins from Assen were only eight. Gassed in Sobibor. They're clever children, my mother said once, when she'd stayed there a few days, they can already read and they haven't started school.

'Has he any children?'

'Yes. How do you know he's married?'

'That's obvious. He's come to Holland with his wife to look at the old place. European Jews who go to America get sentimental from time to time.'

'I went out with him for four years. We saw each other every day. I don't understand.' She banged her fist on the arm of the chair. 'All that time I've been seeing someone else. It's not him. Now I've . . .'

'Now you've nobody.' I became angry. I could never stand her self-pity. I looked at her shoes; gym-shoes with thick soles, clumsy. As if somebody had put them on her without thinking about the legs that went with them. Her stockings were wrinkled. There was green paint on her skirt. I asked: 'Have you ever been to bed with anybody?'

It seemed as if she'd not heard me. Just as well. I now had to think of something else fast. But she said, and her voice sounded measured: 'What a banal way of thinking. What makes you ask that now?'

'I just wondered.'

'What's that got to do with it?'

'Perhaps nothing, perhaps everything. You're twenty-eight.'

'I'm not yet grown up, you mean.'

'You sometimes give the impression. . . .'

As she shrugged her shoulders, she looked at me. I noticed that she did not see me, though. Her mouth moved. I noticed that she wanted to say something and didn't know how to. She clasped her hands together, her stretched thumbs protruding.

'Of course you're right,' she said at last. 'I've not been very lucky when it comes to that. We were very much in love, he and I. When he came to do his homework with me, we were always necking, like you do at that age, kissing and so on. After we'd finished our exams we both thought that something should happen ... that it should happen. The war was approaching and he would be going to America soon.' She paused briefly, stretched, and leant her head against the back of the chair. 'It was Sunday afternoon. My parents had come home late the evening before from a family party and were resting in their room. Leo was with me. He was talking about America, where he would be studying. I was to go too, once he'd finished. But if things went wrong here, I had to get on the boat at once. That's the kind of thing you say then. We sat close to each other. He undid my blouse and bra. He had difficulty with the zip of my skirt and I helped him. It was so natural, it was the only way of saying goodbye, to keep thinking of each other, I thought.'

She rubbed her eyes open. 'Suddenly my mother was in the doorway. We hadn't heard her. I was naked. She looked at us with her face completely rigid. She said nothing and went away immediately. I got dressed and he slunk out of the house. My parents were shocked. They thought that we were good friends; we had betrayed their trust. They were so devout, so naïve. There was no point explaining it to them. It would be better if he didn't come again, my mother said. What difference did it make? Two weeks later I saw him off on the boat. We promised each other, well, what you always promise each other. I was stupid enough not to forget.' She clasped her hands behind her head and looked at the ceiling.

'What about the painter I've seen you with a few times? What's he called?'

'Fred.'

'I honestly thought there was something between you.'

'I liked him. He sometimes came to eat. He had problems. I gave him money for paint and coal. It was the middle of winter.'

'Were you in love with him?'

'No. But I started drawing and painting again through him. I enjoyed helping him.'

'So there was nothing between you?'

'You do go on. I said no.'

'A platonic relationship.'

'He liked me a lot. I noticed that. But he never touched me. First of all I thought he was too shy or that he respected me because I'd talked about Leo. One evening he came to eat. It was very cold. He said his coal was finished and he couldn't face going back to his studio. I said that he could stay if he wanted to. He stayed. I've only got one bed, you know that, a narrow bed. When I got undressed he admitted to me that he wasn't interested in women. "Not in the way you expect perhaps." That's what he said.'

'He was queer?'

'I suppose so. I never noticed. We just lay next to each other. The next morning I gave him money for coal. And afterwards, oh, I wasn't in love with him or anything, I just thought, well . . . what does it matter?'

'He'd have been better off finding a rich friend.'

'In any event that's all there is. You were so curious about my erotic experiences. I never succeeded in anything.'

I stood up. I had to do something. Move about. I walked to the kitchen and held the kettle under the tap. I'd woken up that morning feeling rotten myself. Mark parted the curtains and I saw the grey sky, the rain, a day for staying in bed. I'd had another of my dreams. I was in a big house with my father. This time we didn't go into the rooms but we walked along the corridor down a staircase and came into a cellar. It was cold and the floor was sticky as if someone had spilt tar. My mother lay behind a stone pillar on a table. She was naked and severely mutilated.

Yona had followed me into the kitchen and leant against the doorpost. 'I wonder who's better off, those who have to keep going somehow, who have to pretend that nothing has changed, or the ones who needn't bother any more?'

'Nobody's forcing you.' I poured boiling water into the filter. I deliberately pretended that I'd misunderstood her. 'If you don't feel like something, then don't do it.' The impatient gesture made me put too much water in the filter. It overflowed.

'The way you simplify things, sometimes I think you couldn't care less about it all. But is that so?'

The water seeped slowly through the grains. Foam bubbles appeared at the edges, glistening briefly before they burst.

The woman holds her hands round a glass bowl and looks into the dark, brown sediment. She has red dyed hair which is grey at the parting where it is growing out. She's bald on her crown. Her long earrings remind me of the glass icicles on old-fashioned chandeliers.

The furniture in the little room has been arranged so that you can't walk through it without bumping yourself. The smell of cabbage, dusty velveteen and cat's pee hangs in the air. After a time the woman pushes the bowl away from her and looks at me. Her face is puffy; the pink powder, carelessly applied, lies in patches on her cheeks. 'The persons who you are thinking about are alive,' she says. 'You will see them again soon.'

'Thank you.' I put the coin on the red table-cloth.

Yona took a pepper-pot off the shelf and turned the top.

'I remember my mother getting pepper in her eyes once. We were sitting eating and somehow or other it happened. She panicked. She ran to the kitchen and cried: I'll go blind. My father and I went after her. He took the teapot, poured tea on a towel and bathed her eyes. Later I asked him how he knew that cold tea helped. He smiled and said that at that moment he couldn't think of anything else to do. Act quickly and at the right moment, he always said. He didn't manage to keep to it.'

She put the pepper-pot back.

'Let's not keep harking back to the war.'

'It's all right for you. You take things so damned easy. Specially since you've been in the South. It's as if you shed everything there. I wish I could.'

'The trouble with you is that you've no camouflage. Without that, you can't play the game.'

'Do I have to?'

'Yes, you have to. You have to adapt, everything's normal again.'

Mark's words. I've already started parroting him. We're going to live in another house. A house with a respectable staircase, an electric door-opener, an immersion heater and a bath and a tiled lavatory. We're buying new furniture and new linen and new crockery. Glasses for all kinds of drinks.

I took the cups inside. 'Why didn't you go to Israel anyway? You wanted to go so badly, didn't you? But no, what did you do? You hung around here, wallowing in your own misery, tormenting yourself. And what have you got now?'

'It was an impulse at the time. What would I do in Israel? I'm not cut out for pioneering.' She drank her coffee and abruptly put the cup down as if she'd tasted something not to her liking.

'What else is bothering you?' It was as if she continually circled round something, something for which she could find no words. I couldn't imagine that the return of her friend was the only reason she was so low.

'Nothing,' she said. 'I woke up this morning and wondered what day it was. And at the same time I realized that it didn't make any difference, it was a day like all the rest, it's never any different, there's never a day when I feel there's something to live for. At times I wish we were back in the war. You'll think it absurd, but then we lived for something, every new day, you thought, soon. . . . Now I don't even know what date it is.'

I picked up the morning newspaper from the table. 'It's Friday, 21st April 1950. Flying saucers have been spotted. Ladies' cigarettes are going out of fashion. The international situation is tense.'

'Yesterday I read that they were at it again in West

Germany – Jewish cemeteries destroyed in two places and swastikas chalked up on the headstones. I don't want to know any more.' She jumped up, walked the length of the room and there was a catch in her voice as she said: 'They call it sightseeing. Look darling, over there, that's where my girl-friend lived. He will have pointed up to where my room was.'

'And you torture yourself with it, day in, day out. Stop it, once and for all.'

'Do you know what he asked?' She hadn't even heard me. She came and stood in front of me. There were more paint marks on her skirt, dark crusts. 'He asked me if I would come and stay sometime. I didn't need to worry about the fare.'

'That was nice of him, wasn't it? You really ought to.'

'Really? You must be joking. Do you think he meant it?'

'Why shouldn't he?'

'And if he did, why should I go to America? It's full of anti-Semites anyway. You saw how it was in that film recently. If they realize that you're a Jew, you can't even get a hotel room.'

She fell into the chair and exhaled air with pursed lips as if she was dead tired. It produced in me the same sensation as that evening in hospital when she said they could have let her lie there. The same feeling of impotence. I say the wrong things. I don't communicate. My hackles rise because she's a reminder from beginning to end of something I don't want to be reminded about. I have to do something for her. She expects something of me. Just as Mark does. Say something which makes them feel you love them.

She sat looking at me. I stood up to move away from

her gaze. Who knows, maybe she was here to make it clear to me that she saw me as her only living relative? I would have to talk her out of that idea. I walked to the window and said, without turning round, that she nevertheless ought to think about it.

'About what?'

'About the trip to America.'

'I don't want to.'

'You'll never get the chance again.'

'You want to get rid of me.'

'You'll see something of the world.'

'That's what we thought when we were called up to go to Poland.'

'It'll take your mind off things.'

'You want to get rid of me.'

'You'll get nowhere here.'

'You think I'm a nuisance.'

I leant with my elbows on the window-sill. The rain, the shining asphalt, the rows of windows opposite, I recognized the moment. I'd been through it before. Perhaps it was ten years ago or more. I'm standing in front of the window and looking through the rain at a large building on the other side. A brick façade with innumerable windows. You can see a face here and there, a glimpse of somebody moving behind a curtain. Somebody's looking at me. And I don't dare move an inch.

Yona had walked to the door. She pushed back her hair which was almost dry.

'Are you going?'

'Why don't you say it – I'm a nuisance?'

'Only to yourself. Is there anything I can do for you?'

'I just wanted to talk to you.'

'What are you doing today?'

'Today?'

'Yes, have you got something to do?'

'I don't know. I've kept you. Sorry. You had something to do.'

'Oh, that can wait. I was going to look at the house.'

'It's a good thing you're leaving here.'

I got her raincoat from the kitchen. It was still damp. She put it on and slowly went downstairs. I stood watching her at the stairwell. She was walking bent, her head forwards, her shoulders hunched, as if she was still carrying a rucksack.

'Yona,' I said, 'come and eat this evening.'

She stood still on one of the bottom stairs. For a few seconds I heard nothing; I could no longer see her in the dark doorway to the staircase.

'This evening? I don't know, perhaps. But don't count on me, Sepha.'

I put my coat on again and considered telephoning Mark. I do ring him sometimes. Sometimes I think of some pretext and ask for the foreign editors' section, and then the humming, crackling, ticking of metal on metal, murmur of voices begins and I stand like a child at the back door of a cinema, listening to the noises of a film through a crack.

Mark's voice sounded hurried, abrupt among the clatter of typewriters, and he didn't hear me. He asked if there was anything special and I said no, I said yes, I said that Yona had been.

'Is that why you're phoning me?'

'I'm going to the house now.'

'Haven't you been there yet?'

'No. Yona kept me.'

'Is there anything else?'

'No . . . I . . .'

'Listen, I'm busy. I shan't be home at lunchtime. I'll see you tonight.'

I'd wanted to talk, wanted to listen to the background noises. Say things that just came into my head. Carry on talking without anyone interrupting me. But to whom? Everybody thinks the same, wants to have a say as well, so nothing ever comes of talking.

But not to talk as well, remaining silent for hours, not being forced to look for answers. Why are you saying nothing? You're sitting there as if nothing interests you, as if everything passes you by. Adenauer regrets the anti-Semitic incidents. There's still no threat of war, Truman says. Statues to the Resistance are unveiled. Knighthoods awarded. Collaborators freed. They're going to rebuild the house next door. With stones which have no past. Different people will fancy themselves safe behind the new walls. In a while our house would become unrecognizable too. It was pure accident that they had brought me here. I could just as well have ended up somewhere else, with other people in hiding, another man with whom I lay in bed because there was only one bed. Love is getting used to each other. Once you're used to each other, everything follows its course. Getting up, eating, going out, coming home. It's cold, put a coat on. It's warm, open a window. It's going to rain, make sure you don't get too wet. And the small things, somebody filling your glass, a hand resting on your arm, music which you recognize together, the sound of a voice, warmer than usual, a way of looking.

As I crossed Spui I thought I saw Yona turning into Kalverstraat. I walked more quickly and spotted her in front of the window of a fabrics shop. But it turned out to be a girl who resembled her a lot. The same angular figure, the same stance. I had been so convinced that it gave me a shock. We could have gone to the cinema together. Orson Welles's *The Third Man*. I'd not seen the film yet. I often go to the afternoon performance. What else is there to do? I see the people coming in. Sometimes they walk to their place like robots, feeling the gaze of those already seated. The screen is still blank and you have to look at something. They stretch their backs or hang their shoulders. They don't know what to do with their arms. And even less what to do with their hands. They let them loll at the side of their bodies or shove them in their pockets. Some of them almost stumble at the point where the floor is raked at the first row of the stalls. Women clutch their handbags. As the cinema fills up and the seats around me fill up I'm glad that the lights die, that I can see only the backs of heads below the screen, which shows something happening which is my business only and which I alone sit watching.

'That's nice material.' I was pushed aside and before I turned round I saw myself in the mirror against a background of bright blue flowers. The faces of passers-by seemed expressionless. Under their umbrellas most of them were grey. They walked behind each other, row upon row in bedraggled headscarves and sodden raincoats, in a pointless procession as if someone had told them beforehand that there would be no end to Kalverstraat.

I took the tram at the Munt Tower. It was full, but

I just managed to squeeze in. It smelt of washing that had been soaking too long. A fat man pushed me from behind. His face was bloated and his tiny eyes looked me over while he rubbed the lower part of his stomach against my hips. I stepped backwards, put my heel on his shoe, but that appeared only to encourage him. I couldn't move forwards so I decided to get out after a couple of stops. Thomas's neighbourhood. There was still enough time to go to the house. The gas and electricity men would not have waited for me.

The grey cat was sitting at the top of the attic staircase. She arched her back and pressed her head against my leg. You still remember me? I bent down and stroked her back. She followed me across the dark landing to the door. Before I let the knocker drop, I bent down again and ran my fingers through the loose fur at the back of her head. When the door was opened the animal quickly slipped inside. I walked past Thomas and stood in the middle of the studio.

'Have you changed things around here?' If you go back somewhere after a time, it always looks different from what you had imagined. You know that beforehand. You immediately have a sense of disappointment.

'No, I haven't changed anything. Take your coat off.'

'I only popped in. I just happened to be in the neighbourhood.'

'I'd expected you to come before now.' He hung up my raincoat on a hook on the door.

'I've been busy.'

'What with?'

'Oh, all kinds of things.'

'Are things going well?'

'Yes, we're going to move.'

'What? Are you leaving?'

'We have to. The building's being converted. Some firm is moving in.'

'Where are you going?'

'A house in the south part of the town.'

He laughed. 'A little flat, Sepha?' He stood there, his arms folded, his legs wide apart in front of the door as if he wanted to make sure that I wouldn't leave immediately.

'Something like that.'

'Why don't you sit down?' He pointed to the divan.

I went and sat on a chair at the table and rested my arm on the rough top full of notches.

'Do you want to see the work I've been doing recently?'

'Yes, let's have a look.'

I ran my finger along a notch which ended in a hole to fit a marble. Thomas was busy behind me with his canvases. I would be staggered. He'd completely revamped his work. I wouldn't recognize it. The cat sat hunched on the divan, looking at me. 'Come on, then,' I said and clicked my fingers. She didn't move. She was of course expecting me to come and lie down on the divan so that she could nestle on my stomach like she used to. Sometimes she hooked her claws furiously in my clothes, or drew them over my skin. Once she had leapt on to Thomas's naked back and he had simply left her there. She had rolled around with us. And above, the faces of the children pressed against the frosted glass, only their flattened noses clearly visible. Everybody peeping and knowing. I see them playing in the street as I go round the corner. They're always there. It seems as if they never go to school. Once I'm near to them, they suddenly disappear into a doorway. I can hear them giggling. 'There she is!' I'm wearing a red blouse I made myself from thin material. It has a plunging V neck.

When I come home in the evening, Mark is waiting for me. He interrogates me. 'Who are you wearing that tart's blouse for? Tell me.' He tears it from my body and throws the tatters out of the kitchen window. He hits me on my breasts with the flat of his hand, pushes me against the wall, pulls me towards him. 'Tell me.' I tell him. 'You want to ruin everything. Is this the way we're supposed to carry on?'

'Who started it?'

'Yes, me. I started it. Me. And for you that's a reason to go on and on deceiving me. But get out, if you can't take it. Get out!'

We're standing at the sink. He's torn my bra into pieces as well and I hold my arms crossed in front of my breasts, which are burning from his blows. He's red down to his collar, there are drops of sweat on his forehead, his tie is crooked. He gives me another push. I feel the cold stone edge of the sink against my back.

'Everything seemed just fine when we came back from the South. In the beginning, yes. But you couldn't wait, could you? You just had to hop into bed with any man you met.'

'No, it's not like that. I wanted . . .'

'You had an affair with Karel. Oh yes. Do you think I don't notice these things? With him, and that bloke in Collioure, and every Tom, Dick and Harry.'

'With Karel it was just . . .'

'Spare me the details, thank you. You did it. But I'm not going to take it any longer. I'm damned if I am.'

131

I turned round. Thomas had arranged his canvases along the wall.

'What do you think?' The enormous coloured surfaces stood out sharply against the greying whitewash.

'You have to stand there.' He pointed to the door.

'You've been busy.' I looked from one canvas to the other and they flowed into each other, the hard colours, the fantastic rhythmic patterns, the heavy strokes of the palette-knife, it was all one painting, done by someone who knew what he was doing with paint, but someone who could just as well have put a machine together, made a cupboard or built a wall. It evoked nothing. I mumbled approving words and said I was very surprised. I too had once felt like painting. As a child I'd drawn very well. 'You've got talent,' my mother had said. I'd just turned seventeen when the war broke out. I had a lot of energy, I thought I could do everything. My parents very much wanted me to go to art school. I ended up painting toy cars a vivid blue. The wood was full of knots and so badly glued that half the consignment dropped apart. 'If you've got anything else . . .,' Mark said to the friend who found us jobs like this. That turned out to be making fringes on shawls by fraying the edges. The difficulty was to avoid the wartime material becoming nothing but fringe. I put plaited handles on twisted paper bags and varnished wooden powder-boxes on which somebody else had painted a very primitive flower.

'Do you think I have enough for an exhibition?' He produced some more.

'Oh, yes, certainly.'

'A new direction or not?' He put the canvases around

me as if he wanted to shut me in.

'It's completely different. Very good.' I looked at the glass roof. 'It's dry, I think, I'll have to be off.'

'So soon?'

'I only popped in.'

'Sheltering.'

His shirt was open at the neck. The top button was missing and just a thread stuck out. His corduroy trousers with the belt hung low on his hips. I knew the way in which he undid his shirt with one jerk, let his belt fall to the ground. His clothes in a pile and mine next to them, and then the divan and the faces above us and the children calling out 'They're doing it again.'

There's no difference. Gilbert annoyed me because he laughs uncontrollably when I tell him Mark is coming. 'De quelle marque?' he says, and, 'Pas une marque-mal, j'espère.' We're walking along the pier at Banyuls, a storm is raging, the wind blows my skirt up and he laughs even more loudly and gives the wind a hand. What am I looking for in them? They always want the same thing. They're always occupied with clothes, taking them off and putting them on, off again and on again until every single one of their movements makes me sick because I still keep expecting something else, other gestures, other words, other sensations. I put my raincoat on. The cat jumped off the bed and walked with me to the door, I felt her arched tail stroke along my leg.

The same white nylon curtains were hanging at all the windows. They looked new or as if they had just been washed. A few months ago, short gathered strips had been hanging at the top windows. There were more plants, geraniums and Sansevieria. First of all I'd walked by from the flower shop at the corner and now I was standing in a porch opposite. Why was I looking? What was I expecting to see, all those times I'd stood there watching? The things I'd discovered about the house were the very things I didn't want to see. A bread-man came into the street. He stopped a few metres away from me, opened the back of his van, and secured the door with a hinged metal rod. I smelt the aroma of fresh bread. I saw the piles of loaves, buns, biscuits and cakes. The bread-man eyed me before he rang the bell at one of the houses. I looked up and down the street as if I was waiting for somebody. Behind the door in the porch I heard a voice call something. A high, woman's voice which filled the house, made it alive.

There's a light gaberdine raincoat hanging on the coat-rack, the belt nearly touching the ground. The radio is on, the BBC, Roy Fox and his orchestra.

'My sister, Sepha,' Ellen says. She's smoking a cigarette with a gold filter. There's a heavily built boy next to her on the divan. He has dark, frizzy hair. He raises his hand by way of saying hello. They had evidently moved further apart when they heard me coming in.

'The old folks aren't home, I suppose?'

'Mother'll be here in a minute,' my sister says. 'Have you got a lot of homework?' She crosses her legs and aims the ash from her cigarette into the ashtray on the table next to the divan.

I shrug my shoulders, go to the cupboard, take some

biscuits out of the tin and leave them alone. I eat the biscuits in the hall and walk to the sun porch. Some blue knitting of my mother's lying on a cane chair. The ball has rolled under a plant-stand. I leave it where it is. 'The sun porch suite is still satisfactory,' my father says now and again, a standing joke. He bought it for next to nothing, complete with plant-stand and sewing-box from Mr De Hond, a small, corpulent man with a pointed beard who trades in goods from a closed house. He comes one day to offer us the suite as if it's the chance of a lifetime. If it's not satisfactory, you can always return it. There's a pan on two asbestos rings on the stove in the kitchen. I remove the lid. A large piece of meat is simmering. It smells of onions and tomatoes. I take an apple from the bowl and go upstairs. The umpteenth 'friend'. I can't understand my parents approving of her bringing those boys home. My parents' bedroom door is open. I see my father's slippers under the bed, brown, woollen slippers with flattened backs. There's a calendar with a yellow border hanging on the wall. At the top the year is printed in thick, black letters: **5697**. I go and stand in front of the window in my room and bite into the apple.

The bread-man returned to his van, put two loaves and a malt loaf into his basket and went to the next house. Again he looked at me, longer this time. I retreated further into the doorway and stared ahead of me.

The frosted glass swinging door moves to and fro if you open the front door. The clicking noise of the ball lock. You can see in the lobby whether there are a lot of coats on the coat-rack. They form a dark patch behind the glass. The marble hall floor has sunk a little beside the staircase. Because the sharp ridge had become visible in the hall carpet, my mother has put a piece of thick cardboard there.

Mr De Hond died a year before the war. My father goes to the funeral in his black suit with his silk top hat. The sun porch suite remains satisfactory, the cane simply becomes a little darker and the basketwork on the backs of one of the chairs works loose. My father puts two brass nails in it. 'You need to look after it,' he says.

The bread-man was settling a bill with someone. A woman in a green dress. The malt loaf was still in the basket. What am I doing here? What was I doing in this street, looking at a house like a voyeur?

A house like all the others in the row. I walked through the empty rooms. It smelt of paint and new wood. Every step I made sounded hollow, echoed as if someone was following me at the same pace. Perhaps Yona was here. She knew I was coming. She was hiding somewhere to spy on me, to see how I walked round. She would suddenly appear and say: You see, Sepha, this house isn't the one, either. There's no point in going to live somewhere else as long as you keep taking all your luggage with you, luggage for which there is absolutely no cupboard. Or had she already said it? Only she could say something so melodramatic.

I searched the house but there was nobody. I opened the cupboards, saw the empty shelves, the gas meter, the electricity meter, red wiring. I turned taps on, let the water splash out, listened to it flowing through the pipes. I opened them even more, as if a transfusion had to be administered to the house if it were to come to life. I opened windows at the front and back. A door banged shut because of the draught. An empty tin of paint rolled off a window-sill. I examined everything. Floors on which splinters of wood and bits of fluff were piled in a heap, thresholds and doorposts where the paint was still tacky, door locks, light switches, the chain in the lavatory. There was nothing that did not function properly, nothing that could stop us or which would mean postponing the move.

We are visited by a tall, emaciated man with thin hair lying in strands across his skull. He takes a foot-rule out of his back pocket and taps the walls with it, looking for weak patches. The plaster comes off in clouds. He inspects the kitchen from the hall. He's finished in no time. He nods. 'I've seen everything,' he says. 'It's all coming out. The whole caboodle will be redone.' He shows us forms which state that the premises have been sold to someone who's going to use it for offices. 'We have to have it empty in two months.'

As he walks downstairs we hear him tapping on the walls of the staircase. The outside door jams. He gets it shut only after pulling it a few times. I clean up the plaster and dust the table and the chairs.

'I saw it coming,' Mark says. 'This is just the type of property for a company.'

'How do we find something else?'

'I'll try the newspaper.'

'Still, it's a pity we have to move.'

'All of a sudden you think it's a pity.'

'I'm attached to the neighbourhood.'

'OK, the neighbourhood. . . . But I've heard you say, I don't know how many times, that you want to get away, that you've had enough of this sty.'

Sometimes I hate it. The dingy walls with the plaster falling off, the holes in the floor, the windows that don't close properly, the messy kitchen which I can't keep tidy because we burnt the cupboards in the hunger winter so that there's no place where I can store dishes and food. The evenings I wait for Mark, the nights I'm alone, lying there listening, getting out of bed, going to look outside, to the barge, where a light is still burning, at the woman who always has someone with her. She's in the grocer's when I do my errands. She puts a wad of butter-ration coupons on the counter. Her full blue coat is wide open, even though it's cold. The grocer, a small man with bulbous eyes, who always wears a cap, leers at her breasts protruding in the overtight dress. He calls her 'madam'. He once told me that she was Belgian. She talks broad Amsterdam. She greets me as neighours greet each other and asks how my husband is. 'He always takes his hat off to me so politely,' she says. 'That doesn't happen so often.' Mark doesn't wear a hat but she sees so many men.

I started scratching some of the paint splashes off the windows with my nail-file. A tram stopped at the traffic island opposite the house. People got out, crossed the road hurriedly and all turned the corner simultaneously, as if they belonged together. A little beyond the corner there's a monumental mason. I go past with my father when he goes to get cigarettes. The front garden takes up so much space that you can only just walk two abreast on the pavement. The large ones are at the back, with wrought-iron chains and granite crosses.

The words *rest in peace* have been chiselled out of a white marble block and the letters filled in in black. I walk past quickly and go into the dark shop ahead of my father. When the door closes behind us we are enveloped by the penetrating smell of tobacco. While my father talks with the shop assistant I look into the gas flame to which he holds his cigar. The blue-yellow tongue flickers. I look at it for so long that I keep seeing it on the boxes and chests, on a poster for Christo Cassimis and on the face of the woman who is leaning against the counter with her arms folded. Years later I come back there. I buy a packet of cigarettes. The woman has got fatter. Otherwise nothing has changed. The flame burns on the copper pipe. The gravestones stand in the garden next door as if no one has needed them in all that time. On the other side directly opposite I saw a woman. She held the curtain to one side and looked as if she was shocked by something. She had a narrow, white face. Black hair. A little later she was gone and I no longer knew at which window I had seen her standing.

Children were hanging over the parapet of the bridge throwing paper pellets into the water. A girl was skipping. The rope briefly touched my shoulder. The Zuiderkerk clock struck the half-hour, half-past five. Mark might already be home. But nothing moved behind the windows. He never stood watching as I did.

'I saw your head as I came past just now,' he says.

'What were you doing?'
'Sitting at the window.'
'You never sit there when I'm at home.'
'I'd hardly do it if you were at home.'
'Earning a bit extra on the side?'
'I'm too high up for that.'
'So they have to know, do they?'
'You do, for example.'
'But then I want to right now.'

It happens spontaneously and each time it's different. We also pretend that we've just met each other, that we have met each other in a train between Paris and Brussels. The hot summer makes it easy for us. We throw cushions on the floor and lie naked in front of the open window. And while down below lorries are unloading, traffic jams developing, horns sounding and across the road civil servants are sitting counting, I run my hands over his undulating back and feel the imprint of the coconut matting on his hard buttocks as I press him to me. But sometimes after an embrace, I think it can't last long and I have the same premonition I had in the train coming back, Collioure hours behind us, past Toulouse – as impenetrable as all the towns you go past, girls are bartered, shopkeepers shot down, deserters awaited – and Amsterdam still almost twenty-four hours away; by doing this I try to dismiss the thought that we have to get out, walk across a platform with people who push and people who come between us, so that again we shall have difficulty staying together.

When I came upstairs Mark was standing at the door. 'There you are at last – where were you? I phoned you at least five times this afternoon.'

'Is something the matter?' I tried to think where I'd been and at what time, like somebody looking for an alibi. The morning paper lay open on the table next to the cups from which we'd drunk our coffee. The chair that Yona had moved. I went and sat in it. I'd stood in a square looking at two men on a roof of a tall building working with planks and ropes. I'd watched a boat disappear below me on a bridge and seen it reappear on the other side. There was a clock tower at the end of the canal. The clock showed five to four.

In five minutes school would be out. I'm waiting for my sister who's already in the sixth form. 'You walk on ahead,' she says. 'I'm going with Rudy.'

But I continue walking behind them. She swings her satchel, gives the boy a push now and then, laughs shrilly. The boy is wearing check sports socks. His knees bulge out of them.

'Your sister goes with boys,' whispers the girl who sits next to me on the bench. 'Do you walk behind them to see what they do?'

I shrug my shoulders. 'My mother says I have to come home from school with her,' I say.

'What do they do? Tell me, what do they do?' The child leans towards me, grinning. Two of her front teeth are missing and her rounded tongue sticks through the hole.

'How do I know? Nothing.'

I could have come home later, waited until evening.

Come back in a dark street, in a dark staircase, a twilit room. The darkness provides resting-places, spots where you can get your breath, where you can be semi-invisible. And I felt myself to be all too present in that chair.

'Do you want something to drink, a sherry or something?'

'Give me a gin.'

I'd forgotten to do the errands. There wasn't much in the house and Yona might come to eat. If I was quick I could manage it before six. I stayed where I was. Mark drew a small table closer, put the glasses on it and filled them. He did it carefully. He seemed to need all his concentration to do it.

What had I got to say? I'd popped in to see Thomas. I don't even know why. I'd been on the tram to see the old house and I'd been spotted by the baker. After that the new house. I'd walked back and I'd hung about here and there just looking. A couple of times I'd had the feeling that I'd forgotten to do something, that I still had to go somewhere. For some reason, I couldn't remember what it was.

'Aren't you taking your mac off?'

'Yes. You're right.' I hung it over a chair.

'You look as though you've been walking in the rain all day. Are you cold?'

'A little.'

He poked the stove, put the chair with my coat near to it and pulled my chair towards it too. 'Why do you do it?'

'I like walking in the rain.'

'Did you go to the house?'

'Yes, I didn't see the men. I was too late.'

'And you said you'd be there on time.'

'I phoned you, didn't I, to say that Yona had kept me?'

'What did she want so early?'

'To talk. She's having problems again.'

'What's the matter with her?'

'Why are you suddenly so interested in Yona?'

'I can ask what was the matter, can't I?'

'Oh, there's always something the matter with her. She had one of her fits of depression.'

'When did you get to know her, actually?'

'About five years ago. When I hitched back from Friesland.'

'I've sometimes thought you could be related to each other. Do you think that's strange?'

'I should say so. Do we look like each other, then?'

'No, not at all. And yet . . .'

'There are people who think that all Jewish families are related.'

'I don't mean it like that.'

'Oh, aren't you related to Mrs Cohen? You're the spitting image, that's what made me think that. They don't dare ask "Are you a Jew like Mrs Cohen?" You don't hear the word Israeli any more, it's much too difficult a word, even though you can get round it nicely that way. Because they do want to know whether you're a Jew or not. Why? So they can think, rather him than me.'

He picked up his glass and stared into it. His face was serious. He frowned. I'd expected him to laugh, to make one of his ironic comments, which would lead the conversation off in an entirely different direction. I said, as if we were still talking about Yona: 'She doesn't like you. She had an aversion to you even before she'd seen you.'

'Jealousy.'

'I find it oppressive sometimes.'

He emptied his glass and held it in his hand. The wet patches on my stockings had dried out, they felt stiff, my legs were burning. He put his glass carefully on the table. It made a sharp click. The only sound in the room. I ran my hand over the arm of the chair. It felt rough to the touch. Perhaps I should sand down the arms and restain them. Why doesn't he say anything? I ask.

'What's happened?'

Mark took his cigarettes from his pocket, gave me one, looked for his matches and hurriedly struck one. He drew on his cigarette, inhaling deeply. The lines on his forehead became more furrowed. He had a few grey hairs round his temple. Some men go grey early. Or bald. He has thick hair. He had been blond as a small boy.

'A telex came this afternoon. From Apeldoorn.'

I didn't know anybody in Apeldoorn, not now. An uncle of mine used to live there. We used to visit him on Sundays in the summer. He lived in a big house surrounded by a rambling garden. We used to sit on white benches eating cherries.

'What sort of telex?'

'I happened to be standing there because I was expecting something about the matter with the King in Belgium.'

'Tell me, then.'

'It was about her, about Yona. Her name was there in full.' He bent forward and stubbed his cigarette out on the stove. His arm brushed my leg. 'She was in the train to Apeldoorn. She fell out a few kilometres from the station.' His face had become red from bending

144

forward. 'I immediately phoned the police station in Apeldoorn.'

'Was she . . .'

'It was very bad.' He rubbed his forehead.

'Dead?'

'Dead on impact. The train was going at full pelt.'

Ash had clung to his left trouser-leg, a little above the knee.

'How did it happen?'

'Apparently it happened when she went to the lavatory. They found the door next to it open. Her bag was still lying there. They think it was an accident.'

'Just like when she fell in the water shortly after the Liberation.'

Mark said nothing. He flicked the ash from his trousers.

'This time she succeeded.'

'Nobody said it was deliberate. She might not have felt well and leant on the door handle by accident.'

'She did that once as a child. Her father just managed to save her. Act quickly and at the right moment, he had said.'

'When did she tell you that?'

'A few years ago. Perhaps she didn't plan it in advance. Something might have just come over her. Perhaps she expected somebody would grab her at the last minute.'

'There was a return ticket to Apeldoorn in her pocket.'

'How do you know?'

'The police.'

'What was she going to do in Apeldoorn? She didn't know anybody there, as far as I know. How did they identify her?'

'They found her passport and other papers in her bag.'

'Was her face mutilated?'

He was silent again. I'll hear the details soon. How exactly it happened. The place, the time, the spot where they found her. The statements from witnesses. The words spoken by linesmen and policemen and the men from the local health service over her head, which no longer moved, which was mutilated. I see the doll I let fall out of the window as a child. The head breaks on the pavement and is beyond repair. 'We'll have a new head put on it,' my mother says.

I stood up and put my coat on.

'What are you going to do?'

'I'm going to her room.'

'Shall I go with you?'

'I'd rather go alone.'

The door of the attic was slightly ajar. I'd rung the bell to the storey below, and after the door had been opened, had shouted 'Thank you, I have to go to the attic.'

'She's not there,' someone cried.

The air in the attic was stale, as if a window hadn't been open for days. The divan cover lay carelessly across the unmade bed. There was a plate with a half-eaten sandwich on the corner of the drawing-board. A withered branch in a bottle on the floor caught my coat as I walked past. Clothes were hanging over chairs. There were dirty cups and glasses everywhere. A bowl with rotten apples. A blank sheet of paper had been pinned to the board on the easel and my eyes were continually drawn to it because it stuck out so noticeably in the rest of the interior. I picked up a crayon from a box and hastily drew on the paper. It was blue. I looked for another blue. There were various colours and I used them all, including the blue I'd picked up first. I went on until there was no white left. Afterwards I washed my hands in the sink in the corner. It smelt of damp earth. In the mirror above it my face was distorted by the brown discolourations. They made my nose look longer, my eyes narrower. I moved my head from left to right and backwards and forwards, but I could no longer rediscover the resemblance which momentarily I had thought I could see.

I walked across to the sofa and pressed it. The lumps sagged and produced new lumps as if the bed was full of air. I was just about to sit down when I saw the shoes. They were lying on their sides, half under a cupboard. I pulled them out and stood there holding them in my hand. The heels were askew and the leather on the ankle straps was worn off in some places. I hadn't seen her wear the shoes often. She had bought them in Kalverstraat two years after the Liberation and had to queue for them for hours. As the buckles have to be adjusted slightly, she can't pick the shoes up until the next day. That day there is again a queue. She walks past, goes inside and reappears a short while later from the shop with the box under her arm. A queue of furious women are waiting for her. Someone called out: 'These Jews don't lose any of their cheek.' Another: 'Dirty Jewess – you've already got your nerve back, have you?' And someone else says something about gassing. She remains standing. She thinks perhaps that she has misunderstood. She looks at one of the women, who begins to curse again. A mottled face above a black woollen shawl. She goes across to her. I must do something. I must hit her. I must go back to the shop and get the assistant to tell them that I had to queue yesterday for my shoes. She is pushed aside. A woman tries to tear the box from her hands. They kick her, pull her clothes. She hears something tearing, crouches down and bursts through the queue into an alleyway.

I put the shoes away again and looked at the half-finished painting standing on the cupboard, a self-portrait in misty colours. She hadn't been able to cope. On the drawing-board I found a folder with illustrations for a children's book. When I slid the folder aside, the photographs appeared. They lay there as if she had quickly pushed them out of sight, as if she had been caught looking at them. She had never shown them to me. I thought she no longer had any photographs, that she had lost everything. She looked a lot like her mother, but this face was softer and more regular and the eyes looked straight into the lens with a sort of childlike amazement. The father had a large, bony face with a dark, rounded beard and deep-set eyes behind old-fashioned spectacles. He was wearing a high collar with a widely knotted tie. In later photographs he looked much younger, dressed in a fashionable suit, the beard trimmed short, and always with the same unconcerned smile. And Yona. A schoolgirl in a knitted dress seated between her parents on a settee, her hand in her father's hand, a table with a decorated vase next to them. A Yona who had outgrown herself with long pigtails and sagging knee-length socks. The chin became more aggressive. Standing next to a boy in knickerbockers against a parapet. And again the same boy sitting at a table full of books and documents, the sleeve of his shirt rolled up, a fountain-pen in his hand. *Leo, Summer 1936* was written on the back. He had blond, wavy hair. Yona in a bathing-costume, thin and brown on a beach. Straight as a pole, almost solemn, on the doorstep of a house. Here was the house. The doorstep with the balusters looked like the one by the house next door to us. But the photo was unclear because of a fan-shaped white patch running upwards to the right of Yona, as if some light had got in. It could just as easily have been somewhere else. There were hundreds of doorways like this on the canals. I was glad I didn't know where she had lived, and I wouldn't make any attempt to find out.

I began to put the photographs into some sequence, following chronological order as far as possible so that I could see her growing older. Then I looked at the self-portrait. It didn't look like her at all. But it was already becoming too dark to see it properly. I pulled open the cupboard drawer and found an exercise book under a pile of papers. I took it out. It had a hard brown cover. There was a large letter Y with the Star of David around it on the label. The Y was drawn with black ink, the Star in pencil. Perhaps it was a diary. She might have written in it just yesterday, this morning. At last I'll get to know what had gone on inside her, what her intentions had been when she left here. But I didn't open the exercise book. I replaced it under the papers and closed the drawer.

What had she expected from me when she came to me this morning? Hadn't I given her a chance to say what she had wanted to say? Had she for the umpteenth time wanted to make me feel that I was no less free of guilt?

I walked over to the window. A boy was busy with his bicycle dynamo beside one of the trees. He spun the front wheel and checked to see if the lamp was on. He set off whistling. His rear light wasn't on. A man, bent almost double, was pushing a handcart over the high bridge. Rubbish had been blown together in the corner between the wall of the bridge and the quay, a brown, porridgy layer. I had once asked her if she could swim. 'Yes, at least I can keep myself afloat,' she said. 'I never managed to get a diploma.' What had she managed, then? This? And who could say whether she wanted this? Actions sometimes precede the will. Before you want to, you've done something which is irrevocable.

It was now so dark in the attic that I could no longer make anything out at the back. I heard someone coming up the stairs. Clumping. The door creaked. It was Mark. He stood in the light of the doorway.

'It's dark in here. What are you doing? Have you found anything?'

'No, nothing.'

'Isn't there a light here?'

'Yes.'

'Where's the switch?'

'Don't bother. There's no need now.'

'Are you coming? Are you coming home?'

'Yes, I'm coming.'

I removed the key from the inside of the lock, closed the door and pushed the key into my pocket.

As we walked over the bridge, I looked up at the attic windows. The glimmering panes beneath the dirty white eaves. I stood still because the shutter between the windows had escaped me, a black shutter with a hoist above it. But I was turned round by Mark. With his arm around my shoulders he pulled me away into a side-street where it was dark and where, at that very moment, the street lights went on.

DATE DUE

FIC   Minco

WITHDRAWN

92-13   7/92